"What is it, Aiodhán? _____
straight with me and I _____

He slumped into the oversize chair she'd found him in when she awoke. Had she ever seen the man sit down? Once, when he laced up his shoes after their... night together. Beyond that, he was a workhorse, dragging the rest of them behind him. Anxiety jumped atop her nerve endings like they were springs.

"Are you seeing anyone, Emilia?" he asked. Why did his face look pained as he asked the question? "Or have you since we—"

The abrupt shift in topic was jarring.

"Pardon me, what business is that of yours?"

"I didn't mean to hurt you with that question. I just need to know, as your doctor."

"No," she whispered. "I'm not seeing anyone and haven't since you and I on that first night."

Aiodhán looked relieved and conflicted at the same time, but unease lingered around his eyes.

When he didn't continue, she spoke up. "Do you mind telling me why that's related to my diagnosis?"

"You're pregnant, Emilia. We're...*we're* pregnant."

Dear Reader,

I don't know about you, but I've always been curious about the world that royals inhabit and how royals would fare in the day-to-day most of us experience. I thoroughly enjoyed playing with that idea in Aiodhán and Emilia's medical-meets-royal love story. As it turns out, royals aren't all that different from us.

Princess Emilia is nursing a wounded heart—not just from her broken engagement but from the secret her ex shared before they split. She leaves her home country, hoping to find balance between her loyalty to the crown and her dreams of practicing medicine. Aiodhán's hopes are simpler—by working and keeping everyone at arm's length, he can avoid the inevitable loss that comes with caring.

We know that's not true, though! When love is ready, it'll find even the most timid of us wherever we're hiding, and isn't that the hope we all carry? So dive in and enjoy this tale of seeming opposites as they find a way in this modern world together, despite the challenges that try to pull them apart.

Drop me a line and let me know what you think on X, Instagram or Facebook, or by email at kristinelynnauthor@gmail.com.

Kristine Lynn

NINE MONTHS TO
MARRY THE PRINCESS

KRISTINE LYNN

MEDICAL ROMANCE

Harlequin® MEDICAL ROMANCE

Recycling programs for this product may not exist in your area.

ISBN-13: 978-1-335-94302-6

Nine Months to Marry the Princess

Harlequin Enterprises ULC
22 Adelaide St. West, 41st Floor
Toronto, Ontario M5H 4E3, Canada
www.Harlequin.com

Printed in U.S.A.

Hopelessly addicted to espresso and HEAs, **Kristine Lynn** pens high-stakes romances in the wee morning hours before teaching writing at an Oregon college. Luckily, the stakes there aren't as dire. When she's not grading, writing or searching for the perfect vanilla latte, she can be found on the hiking trails behind her home with her daughter and puppy. She'd love to connect on X, Facebook or Instagram.

Books by Kristine Lynn

Harlequin Medical Romance

Brought Together by His Baby
Accidentally Dating His Boss
Their Six-Month Marriage Ruse
A Kiss with the Irish Surgeon

Visit the Author Profile page at Harlequin.com.

To Cindy.

Thank you for helping make my writing fairy tale
come true! You're the best agent a gal could ask for.

**Praise for
Kristine Lynn**

PROLOGUE

EMILIA DE REYES stared down the long wooden bar. Each seat was occupied, the screams of laughter deafening, the rock and roll competing for space in each patron's eardrums. She took a deep breath and squeezed between two towering, bulky humans, trying to find enough real estate to flag the bartender down.

Neither gave Emilia a glance. She smiled.

This is amazing. I'm actually invisible.

A bartender materialized.

"Whadaya having?"

She glanced above him at the menu outlined in chalk—*chalk! How truly American!*—and thought of her "list."

"How about the Big Sam and an old-fashioned?"

The man nodded and disappeared. He was fully what she expected to find in a hipster bar like the one she'd chosen, with a loose bun piled atop his head and what might pass as a beard smattering his chin.

This whole scene—from the noise to the scent of something fried and delicious to the people casually dressed in off-brand clothing—was exactly what she'd hoped for when she'd chosen Minneapolis, Minnesota, for her obstetrics residency in the United States. When she'd dared to hope, that was.

When her stepmother had stopped seeking fertilization treatments after too many failed pregnancies, Emilia had worried that her let's-turn-the-princess-into-a-well-rounded-queen-to-the-people trip was *off the table*, to use an American turn of phrase. In a moment, she'd gone from hopeful that her life could be *guided* by royal protocol, rather than dictated by it, to *resigned*.

Her father and stepmother would never have a child of their own. Which meant…

Emilia was the sole heir to the Zephyranthes throne. And her dreams of picking a so-called passion project to follow for two years, as all Zephyranthian nobility did, was likely off the table. Emilia's health and safety could no longer be risked.

A patron at the bar whooped when some athlete competing in an American football match crossed over a line on a field. Emilia smiled, feigning interest in the television above her. At least one good thing had come from Luis's betrayal and her biggest mistake being plastered across the front pages of every European newspaper: he'd given her an out.

All that negative media coverage and her sudden disappearance from the limelight would have made it seem as if she were running away. Instead, her situation was rebranded as the start of her "queen in training" preparation.

It'd worked, too. Especially when the media got wind of what she'd chosen as her passion project. She'd be working toward a medical specialty in obstetrics in America, helping women like the late queen, who'd died in childbirth. She felt moderately guilty for capitalizing on her mother's death two decades earlier, but Emilia was also healing from a fresh betrayal there as well. There was so much her mother hadn't told her… So much she'd been blind to since she'd only been seven when her mother passed away. Now, thanks to Luis, all her past was on a world stage for everyone to read about in the scandal pages.

And Luis himself? Well, he was part memory, part heartache, and full regret at this point. He was banished from Zephyranthes, at least.

Her engagement to Luis might've left her with a decent heartbreak, but it gave her a chance to pursue more than just a passion project. Much more.

She *loved* medicine, and in that brief moment after her father had remarried and started trying to have more children, Emilia had allowed herself to imagine what life as a royal physician might have been like. But now she was back to her role as Heir Apparent, Queen-in-Waiting.

At least she had an American hamburger with *bacon*, not to mention a whiskey drink on the way. *Check and check.* Two things crossed off her list before she'd even finished unpacking.

This was a good idea, coming here.

The shout from the crowd was louder than the rock music; someone must have done something outrageously stupid or heroic on the TV. Her smile grew.

Emilia's stay would be short-lived, a mere two years, but she didn't mind. She loved her country, found honor in her duty, and would appreciate going back to meet the needs of the people counting on her.

But anonymity was a welcome respite. Well, sort of.

She stole glances toward the door. There, leaning against a post, was Chance, her father's answer to keeping her safe while allowing her to complete her OB residency in America. Without a drink of his own, and in all black, he looked more bar bouncer than patron.

Likely, he thought this assignment beneath him. Still, he could loosen up and try to enjoy being outside the gated walls of the castle. Wasn't he happy to be out from the stifling duties of her father's chief adviser?

When a large, male form almost brushed against her at the bar, her smile turned to shock at a stranger being this close to *her*. With Chance mere feet away. Out of the corner of her eye, she noticed Chance close the distance, but she shook her head. She was okay. No, she was better than okay.

I'm not in the castle anymore, am I?

Emilia tried to take in the man who'd somehow made the seas part for him, but he was too close and too tall—well over two meters. The gray sweater he wore swept across her skin, tickling it. It was soft, *expensive*. His broad chest and strong arms pressed against the fabric but didn't strain it. The sweater had been tailored for him—she'd recognize that kind of craftsmanship anywhere.

How interesting to find it in middle America at a local bar.

The muscles in the man's torso extended to his neck, his jaw, his cheeks.

But that's all she could see.

What she *felt* was another story altogether. She'd never been this close to a *man*—other than Luis, who hardly earned the right to be called as much. Luis had been attractive in the basic sense of the word, but masculine? Nothing like the man beside her.

She inhaled deeply, the scent of spicy soap overwhelming her senses. Romance had never been, nor wouldn't ever be, an option, if for no other reason than the crown didn't allow it. Not in the conventional sense.

Her royal obligations included a marriage of convenience that would benefit her country, which was sort of romantic if she thought about the centuries of tradition that supported the ceremony she'd partake in when she returned to Zephyranthes.

Then again, her father and stepmother hadn't expressly told her she couldn't pursue a *fling*.

In that case, a man as intoxicating as this one might make the top five list of things to do in America. Modern decrees had relinquished outdated policies about a princess's virtue, which Emilia hadn't taken advantage of. Yet.

As the velvety voice of the man next to her ordered his drink—something with *sour* at the end of it—a pooling of heat sank past her abdomen and into the place she longed to be touched.

Apparently, the things she'd learn on this trip wouldn't all be within the hospital walls.

No sooner was she handed a glass of amber liquid did the hulk of a man back into her, spilling at least a third of it. And he didn't even bother to turn around.

Desire turned to ice, heavy and cold in her stomach. She tapped his shoulder. "Excuse me." He dipped his gaze at her angry words. "You spilled my drink."

She raised her chin and was met by a piercing gaze the same slate gray color as his sweater. The full force of his power and nonchalance was something she was all too familiar with in the world she'd left behind.

"I apologize. I didn't realize. Can I replace it?" he asked.

"No, thank you. This will be plenty, I'm sure. But you could be more careful. Someone might've been hurt."

"Were you? Hurt?" He handed her a napkin but didn't turn away.

"No." Her pulse beat loud in her ears. "Not this time."

"Good."

Emilia held his gaze. When his brows lifted in appreciation, she swallowed, her throat dry. All moisture in her body had fled south, it seemed.

"You're beautiful," he said.

"I know," she replied, crossing her arms over her chest. It wasn't as if she was unaware of her physicality. She was raised to consider its importance above almost everything else in her life. Yet, to see its effect without thought or care for what being caught gazing at a *princess* might do to his reputation—his *life*—was a heady thing indeed.

She also knew she'd chosen wisely when it came to the slinky jade green shirt with thin straps exposing her toned shoulders and her slim-cut black jeans. The former highlighted the jeweled green slivers in her eyes, the latter her figure.

He laughed, then, his stoic demeanor gone. "Where are you from?"

"Why do you assume I'm not from here?"

"The accent, for one."

She shrugged, conceding to that observation. She'd worked hard to learn American English, but every now and then, even she heard the stray *theta* from her native Zephyr—similar to Spanish—that slipped through into speech.

"That's fair. And the rest?"

His eyes sparkled with recognition, and awareness prickled her skin.

"You don't fit in here," he said with a finality that left no room for an opposing opinion. A stab of something familiar and unwanted pulsed in her chest.

"Neither do you," she shot back.

She'd tried for *confident* and come up short. That was the problem, wasn't it? She didn't belong anywhere. Too wild for her royal existence, too proper for much else. If it weren't for years of training, the worry she couldn't be the princess Zephyranthes needed would have devoured her a long time ago.

He laughed again. "Trust me, it's a compliment.

But yeah, this place isn't my normal scene. I'm supposed to be meeting a friend in a bit."

"A friend?" Why did a thread of jealousy tug at her heart? This man—this handsome stranger—didn't owe her anything.

"My buddy, Brian." Unexpected relief cut the thread. "But you still didn't answer my question. Where're you from?"

"Europe." She kept her answer simple, alluding to the story she, her parents, and Chance had worked out. It was tenuous, but at least they could count on Luis's silence from wherever he'd slunk off to. They'd paid handsomely for it.

"Spain?" he asked.

She shrugged, allowing the common misconception. Their language and culture were similar enough, buying her even more anonymity.

"*Encantado*," he said, dipping his chin. "*Me llamo* Aiodhán."

The accent and greeting weren't as fluid as Zephyr, but she didn't fault him for that. Hearing something close to her native tongue from his lips was thrilling. Whiskey did the job the desire started, and she had the sudden urge to give into the heat building at her core.

When she got bumped from behind this time, she careered into the wall of muscle in front of her. The arms that held her up were strong, warm, and wholly tempting. Kind of like the rest of the man.

Not yet, and not him. Besides the obvious—he was the first American she'd spoken to—she couldn't escape the feeling wafting off the handsome stranger. Aiodhán was trouble, and until she was sure if it was the good kind or not, she'd best keep her distance.

"Emily?" the bartender asked, breaking the spell she'd fallen under while under Aiodhán's gaze. She nodded. The nickname was one more buffer between her and her royal reality. Once someone associated her with the...*family obligations* she had back home, she would no longer be Emilia, woman and physician. Just *Princess* Emilia.

The bartender held out a brown bag. Perfect timing. Flirting with the stranger next to her had diverted her attention from the pangs of hunger she felt, but barely.

"Emily, huh?"

She straightened her shoulders, tossed her hair back.

"Yes. Well, nice to meet you, Aiodhán." She held out her hand to bid him good-night, but he ignored it. Fine. She turned to leave despite his breach of etiquette.

"You been here long?" She stopped short. What would five more minutes of chatter cost her?

"I haven't. This is my first day here, actually."

"Welcome to Minneapolis," Aiodhán said. "What brought you here?"

"Work. I start a new job Monday." The less he knew, the better. Only the CEO of the hospital system she was completing her residency at was aware of her real name, her credentials. And it would remain that way for the next twenty-four months.

His eyes narrowed. "Have you ever been to Minneapolis before?"

She shook her head. "It's a beautiful city, though." Nothing like the centuries-old spires in the center of Cyana, but modern, fresh, *new*.

"I like it. And I'm thinking you need a tour guide."

"Is that right?" The food bag hung at her side, all but forgotten under the intense gaze of this stranger.

"It is. How about after you dive into that burger we get you acclimated? As a resident downtown expert, I'm your guy."

"How are you such an expert?" she teased. It felt good. Freeing.

"I'm doing a project downtown with a new building, so I had to do market research. All boring stuff, but it did give me one gem." The look he sent her was primal, filled with adventure. Her skin prickled with awareness. "It's a fun place with some great music if you'd like to join me."

"What about your friend?"

He shrugged. "He'll live without me for a night."

"Well, I don't know you," she said, worrying aloud.

His smile didn't waver.

"That's why people go on dates, generally. To get to know each other."

A thrill whispered through her. *Dating*. What a wholly American—and ordinary—thing to do. It'd never actually occurred to her.

Didn't I choose to pursue my residency in the United States so I could learn about other cultures that might impact the way I lead one day?

Not exactly. However, she *was* there to heal from heartache and take on a passion project. Maybe there was another way to look at those edicts.

"Okay," she said, a smile working its way across her face. "I'm interested. But only after I've devoured this burger. I'm absolutely starving."

Aiodhán's laugh was throaty and thick.

"I'd never dream of keeping a woman from a meal." He swallowed the contents of his drink then placed the empty glass on the bar. The gleam in his eye was positively wicked, with a hint of feral desire she recognized from the men who'd coveted her on their supervised courting outings, men like Luis. Only this man wasn't aware of the fortune or title she carried like invisible, gilded baggage on her shoulders. He whipped out a credit card and waved at the bartender. "I'll take all this, too."

"You don't have to—"

"Consider it a welcome drink and dinner. Just sit back and enjoy."

Well, this is a pleasant surprise. For obvious reasons, she was usually left fronting the cost of all dinners out.

Another pleasant surprise? Aiodhán cleared the way for her to dive into her food, which she did with reckless abandon. Not one worry about dabbing her lips with a cloth napkin or if she looked silly crossed her mind. Aiodhán wiped a smudge of ketchup from the corner of her mouth, but otherwise let her eat in peace.

"Ready to go, Emily from Europe?" He leaned in close enough that the spice from his soap tickled her nose. She inhaled deeply, wanting to remember this scent—the scent of her first American date. Her first *real* date.

Excitement rolled through her chest, even as she allowed Aiodhán to believe she was someone other than who the world knew her as. She stole a glance at Chance. The plan forming in her mind was almost unfair to the stoic, frowning grump of a man, but that didn't deter her from putting it into action. After all, hadn't she slipped his watch countless times in Cyana as a child? She'd learned a few tricks since then.

"I'm ready, Aiodhán from Minnesota," Emilia said. "Let's go."

Her heart beat wildly as reality hit her. Yes, she'd been placed back at the top of the line of succession. But she was also free for *two whole years*. Sudden desperation for adventure beat in her chest. A date with an attractive man she'd met at a local bar seemed just the trick. The rest—her dream of working with new moms and women who needed her help to have the families they craved—was on the horizon. And the sun would rise on it tomorrow.

Right now, she was focused on the man taking her hand in his leading her out of the bar and into the magic of the unknown.

CHAPTER ONE

EMILIA APPLIED A thin layer of gloss on her lips before appraising her look in the mirror. It reminded her of the last time she'd applied makeup—the night she'd slept with the hot American she met in the bar two weeks prior. She shuddered but smiled, memories of the most delicious night of her life still tingling her lips, no matter how much gloss was painted on.

No time for that now. Even if she couldn't forget the spectacular way he'd wielded her body like a surgical instrument of pleasure, those memories stood in the way of what mattered. Namely getting ready for her first day of work, acclimating to this new life, and healing while she had the space to do so.

Oh, and finding a decent place to put on her makeup.

She'd moved into her apartment a week ago and still couldn't figure out the dimmer switch in the bathroom. Had she overdone the blush on her cheeks? Like many aspects of her move so far, she was both frustrated by small details and overjoyed at the freedom they represented. Sure, it would have been nice to have her consorts and lady's maid to assist her in getting ready, and ooh, she missed her Scandinavian LED makeup mirror.

But then again, wasn't it delicious to stay up all evening reading a *romance* novel instead of a foreign policy text by a stuffed-shirt scholar? She'd deal with poorly lit rooms for that unique pleasure.

This apartment *was* a cut above decent, considering they'd only decided Minneapolis was an option for her residency two days before she flew out. The hospital had accommodated her, no questions asked. But housing…? That had been a different story altogether.

Emilia giggled, recalling the king's beet-red cheeks as he was given the runaround by an apartment manager for luxury apartments near the hospital.

"I don't care if you're King George. I don't have anything for ya."

"King George has been dead for three-quarters of a century," he'd huffed. Emilia had wondered whether her father was more upset about the lack of options afforded a man of his position or that he was compared to a deceased ruler of a different country. "Do you have anyone more qualified than you to assist me?" he'd asked.

God love her father, but he wasn't immune to the blinders his power put on him. It was part of why this whole trip was so important to Emilia. She didn't want to get to the throne only to discover she didn't know her place or her heart's values. How could she be expected to lead without perspective and context for the rest of the world's issues?

"I hope this is worth it, Emilia. I don't want to see you hurt again," the king had said once a suitable apartment had been secured.

"It will be," she'd assured him. And so far, that was true, if only because it separated her from her mother's story, while giving her time to grieve. Not just the lie she'd been fed by everyone, including her father, but the life she'd had stripped away when her lineage had become more important.

Emilia's stepmother and the king had nurtured her dreams to practice medicine, but it always came secondary to trying for another heir. Emilia understood. A baby had been *their* dream, just as hers was making sure women had the kind of care denied her birth mother, despite being pregnant with the future prince. Her death had rocked Emilia's childhood.

It had also left a chasm of grief in her father's chest, in the country's memory, but both had been replaced. Her father's grief turned to love—deep love—with a woman in a graduate program at a Zephyr university he met at a summit. The country liked the new queen but kept Emilia's mother in its heart. That is, until Luis had somehow unearthed the unthinkable.

The baby her mother carried hadn't been the king's.

If Emilia had learned that as an innocent seven-year-old, she might've taken the news differently. But mere months ago? When she'd looked up to her mother her whole life, even altering her career choice to honor her mother's sacrifice?

The country's shock was nothing to Emilia's. Nor was their grief. Emilia was still reeling. She'd always assumed her parents had been happy. What else didn't she know?

Here, four thousand miles from her sandy shores, she could pick through these thoughts without the scrutiny of an entire country.

Emilia sighed, slipping on her tennis shoes. The one thing finding out about her mother hadn't shifted was Emilia's love of medicine. Learning bathed her grief in the salve of knowledge, tucked it away between the covers of science texts, in the conversations with her professors at the Royal Zephyranthes Conservatorium Medical School.

"It's finally here," she whispered to herself. Tucking an errant strand of hair behind her ear, she grabbed her phone and headed for the door. "Don't mess this up."

In the elevator on the way down from the penthouse suite, she checked her messages.

One from her stepmother, wishing her luck, and… that was it.

What exactly am I looking for?

Regret opened wide in her throat. She hadn't given Aiodhán her phone number, and why should she have? They'd shared a passionate night and nothing more.

In her world, marriage, romance, and love were mutually exclusive, but the latter two? They just weren't in her cards if nothing could come of it. Hope had buoyed her on more than one occasion, but hoping to find what her father and stepmother had was too much to put on the universe. She was lucky to be here, to study medicine, and that was enough.

Still, she hadn't counted on the after-effects of sleeping with Aiodhán. Her skin tingled with memory where he'd caressed it, her hands itched to move across the continents of flesh he'd laid open for her. Her body craved his, plain and simple.

And, like all tragedies, she didn't even have a last name to cyberstalk the man, or at least put Chance to the task of tracking him down.

Thank goodness, too. The elevator doors opened to her future—the lobby of the hospital. Who had time for a love affair when *life* was hers for the taking? And with a very definite timeline?

A smile bloomed on her face as the cool Minneapolis wind whipped her ponytail into a dance. She was going to learn and practice obstetrics in the United States. And under a pilot program called the Gold Fleece Foundation that had begun in LA for women who couldn't afford good care, no less.

Finally. Her future felt like *hers* for the first time. She tried not to think about it being the last, as well.

Inside the foyer she'd just entered, the only word Emilia could come up with was *vivo.* This place was *alive*.

The stories-high pale green walls surrounded a miniature city that pulsed with energy. People in different-colored scrubs—maybe delineating their departments within the hospital?—rushed across the sepulchral space as if their worlds lay on the other side of whatever doors they passed through. People like *her*, there to learn to save lives, or already well on their way to doing just that. It was loud, chaotic, but with a measure of reason and pacing that Emilia recognized. Everyone and everything had a place and a role. Stepping into her own would be adding another cog to the wheels that made this place run. Emilia gazed in wonder, a sense of something calm settling over her, despite the frenetic energy whizzing around her.

Home. She was home.

No sooner did that realization wash over her than a tap on her shoulder roused her from Minneapolis General's bustle.

It was followed by a bright voice with an accent different than the one she'd heard around the city. Those were all long *O*s, a lilt at the end of each sentence, turning them into questions. This was thick and sweet, a cup of sugary tea.

"Y'all new here, too?"

Emilia whirled around, a smile on her face. The *too* warmed her. So did the spritely blonde greeting her with wide blue eyes. There were a few other folks who looked like they were waiting for orientation as well, but they were all on their phones, serious expressions pinned to their faces.

"It's my first day. Are you part of the residency program as well?"

"Sure am. Straight from Georgia. I'm Bridget. Hoping to work in peds." *Georgia.* That explained it. After reruns of *The Golden Girls* as a motherless teen with too much time on her hands, Emilia recognized the southern accent.

"Emilia. Obstetrics. Nice to meet you."

"Same. Obstetrics, huh? No joke messing around with two lives at a time. I like it."

"Thanks. The Gold Fleece program is one of the best, so I'm feeling terribly lucky."

"I've heard the same. Say, where's that fancy accent from?" Bridget asked her.

"Um… Spain," she said, sticking to her lie by omission from the other night. "I've only been here two weeks."

"Wow. And you didn't want to stay there with all the Mediterranean men? I've been here since last Thursday doing my onboarding paperwork, and aside from the head of general surgery, it's like the Sahara desert—dry of anything resembling life."

Emilia laughed. "Trust me, the men over there aren't as interesting as you'd think."

An image of Luis's cold sneer flashed in her vision. Her only consolation from being duped by such a weasel was knowing he'd been vetted by the crown as well and, until proven otherwise, had passed inspection. At least he'd sold their secrets to the press before she'd actually walked down the aisle.

She shivered. It would be hard to trust the next man her father chose for her, but she knew he'd be a thousand percent more cautious. Neither her nor her country could survive another betrayal.

Too bad the only man she had trusted and felt

safe with was the one she'd shared her bed with two weeks ago.

Aiodhán. A shiver ran up her spine as she recalled his hands sliding over her skin, his tongue tracing her anatomy, the way he thrust into her… She might not have had any *physical* experience with men before Aiodhán, but she couldn't imagine it got better than the night—and very early morning—she'd spent with him.

She shook the heat of the memory away.

"Anyway, I'm not here to date."

"So what *are* you here for?"

Emilia smiled, her focus on a woman with a gash over her left eye being led away by a young man in blue scrubs. She thought she'd figured out the color coding in the past few minutes of watching medical staff move in and out of the lobby, where they were told the residency coordinator would meet them. Pink was maternity, black for surgery, blue for the ER, and yellow for pediatrics.

"I want to work while I still can, travel if there's any time, and," she said, "have as much fun as possible. Dating would only get in the way of that."

Bridget eyed her through thick, fake lashes.

"Good," she finally said. "I need a wingwoman and if you're staying off the market, there's more hope for regular-looking people without Mediterranean accents."

"I'm happy to help," Emilia said, tossing Bridget a sly wink. "Maybe we can start at this local bar. I met an absolutely beautiful man there the other night."

"We're gonna be fast friends," Bridget said, laughing and throwing an arm around Emilia's shoulders.

Emilia warmed at the idea of a friend. She'd never had anyone she trusted enough to let down her guard with.

"I'm glad you're enjoying yourselves, but I'd like to get started if that's okay with you?"

Emilia whipped around. The voice washed over her with eerie recognition.

Sure enough, the face staring back at her was as familiar as it was unnerving. Largely because she couldn't reconcile the strong shoulders, broad chest, and tree-trunk thighs draped in pale blue scrubs that brought out hints of robin's-egg blue in his eyes she'd missed the other night under poor bar lighting. The man standing before her was all rough edges and steely gaze, where he'd been soft and inviting mere days before.

"Aiodhán?" she whispered.

"*Emily*, is it?" His pupils dilated, but his lips remained pressed tight. The night they'd shared may not have meant enough to warrant a reaction from him, but heat singed her skin.

She shook her head. "Um, Emilia, actually."

"Hmmm." He looked away, but the heat from his stare still burned where it had caught her in the small, but meaningful, lie.

Emily was the name she'd picked for when she met people outside the hospital, but of course, everyone here would be aware of her name, if not her title. But other than the withering stare, he didn't comment.

That didn't change the way he stood over her. In her space. Taking up all the oxygen in the room.

"Like I was saying," Aiodhán continued, ignoring her, "I'm Dr. Adler, the chief of general surgery. I'll be running the clinical rotations, which means I'll get to know all of you in time, but right now, I'd like us to get started. Follow me."

Dr. Adler. Chief of Surgery. All things she should have known about the man before sleeping with him. If only they'd spent more time talking and less time tearing each other's clothes off.

Emilia shivered.

"You know this guy?" Bridget hissed under her breath. "He's the general surgery doc I was telling you about. The only one hot enough to imagine breaking the rules for in this place."

"What rules?" Anxiety crept over Emilia's skin.

"You know, the *don't sleep with the boss* rules in every place of employment. Especially an ER where we'll spend sixteen hours a day together." Bridget laughed, but not one thing about this situation was humorous. How could Emilia have known he was her *boss*? Or the rules of employment when she hadn't been allowed to have a job until now? "Can you imagine if you slept with him and then had to see him at work every day? Awkward..." Bridget sang the last word.

Oh, God. That's exactly what Emilia had done, and *awkward* didn't begin to cover it.

Aiodhán—Dr. Adler—led them through the lobby to a room with metal lockers and restrooms.

"This is your break room and where you'll store your personal belongings during your shift. Take the next five minutes and change into the scrubs we've laid out for you, and then we'll continue our tour."

He left the locker room, and a collective sigh of relief escaped all of the residents' lungs. With the exception of Emilia's, that is. Pressure built up in her chest, making it ache.

"That guy's intense," one resident said. Others echoed similar sentiments.

"I thought he was hot. And you know him?" Bridget asked.

Emilia shook her head, willing her skin not to flash red with her newest lie. Oh, she knew the guy. *Intimately.*

"He looked like someone I knew, but he couldn't be that man—he was sweet and kind, and Dr. Adler doesn't seem like those adjectives describe him."

A small truth hidden in the bed of lies.

"Too bad—I kinda wish you could make a personal introduction. Adler is *fine.*"

Emilia finished getting ready before the others but didn't dare step out into the hallway alone. Not when *he* was out there.

When Bridget was dressed, Emilia followed her out. She glanced up and caught Aiodhán staring at her for the briefest of seconds before his gaze shifted to the others. That small blip of recognition was all she saw reflected in his eyes before casual nonchalance took over. Anger, she could have understood—she'd lied to him, after all. But he was acting as if he barely recalled meeting her.

Her own anger surfaced.

Hadn't he lied to her, as well? He'd said he was working on a building downtown. *Ha!* This only barely qualified.

Please let this be some sort of cosmic joke. That she'd never set foot in that bar two weeks ago.

Except it had happened. All of it. Aiodhán Adler was her boss, and she had to spend the next two years with the man while he pretended he didn't recognize her.

She'd hoped for anonymity, but was she really that forgettable?

A flood broke through the dam holding Emilia's emotions back. Heat pressed against the back of her eyes, and her chest pulsed with regret. She'd slept with her boss and all but ruined any chance of being known for her medical aptitude. That, and she didn't have a single person she could ask for advice.

No, this was her mess, and she was responsible for cleaning it up.

Sadness washed over her, replacing the adventurous thrill from earlier.

Oh, my goodness. What have I done this time?

CHAPTER TWO

A<small>IODHÁN</small> A<small>DLER</small> <small>STORMED</small> down the hallway. His steps were heavy, but not as weighty as the pressure building in his limbs, his chest, his head. Shaking his head at the charge nurse who seemed bent on getting his attention, he bypassed the beeps and trills of the nurses' station.

"I'll be back in a sec."

He just…he needed a *moment* to catch his breath, to think through how to handle this…*situation*. When he rounded the corner and found the first on-call room unoccupied, he breathed out a heavy sigh.

Emily. In *this* hospital. In *his* program.

Emily isn't even her name.

Fine. Whatever. Emilia-freaking-de-Reyes. He might have to call her something different, but the effect on his breathing, his memory, his heart was the same.

He snatched a pillow off the on-call bed and groaned into it. He'd let a moment of weakness and that damned accent snake under his defenses and ruin a two-year streak of saying no to his basest desires.

And, hell, was he paying for it now.

He inhaled deeply, letting the cool air in the quiet room calm his racing pulse. After the urge to run for the Canadian border passed, he placed the pillow back on the bed, straightening the sheets while he was at it.

Aiodhán fished out his phone and dialed.

"You know that woman I told you about?" he asked when his best friend answered.

"Hello to you, too," Brian said, laughing. In the background, Aiodhán heard another laugh he recognized.

"Tell Mallory *hi*."

"Ad says *hi*," Brian said. "She says *hi* back. And that she forgives you for skipping out on half our reception."

"I made it the whole way through the ceremony." He might not understand the desire to date, fall in love, and then commit to someone who could wreck your world if they left—by choice or chance. But Brian and Mal were his best friends.

"Anyway, what's up? You called about some woman?"

When Mallory snorted with laughter in the background, he grimaced.

"Can you take me off Speaker?"

"Sure thing." Aiodhán heard the door close on Brian's end. "Dang, man. This must be serious if you're calling me on my honeymoon and don't want Mal to hear."

"It's serious, but not like you think. Remember the woman I met at the bar that night?"

"When you blew off my bachelor party? Yeah, I recall."

"I didn't blow it off. I was there."

"For two minutes at the beginning to tell me you were leaving, and without the cigars you promised."

"Again, I'm sorry, but—"

"It couldn't be helped," Brian said, echoing the words from Aiodhán's text, sent from the elevator of his apartment when he'd kissed Emilia. But Aiodhán could hear the smile in his voice.

"No. It couldn't." Even now, he could feel the pull she'd had on him that night. It was magnetic and untamed: dragging himself away would have been like shoving a dead vehicle across the banks of Lake Superior. And worse? He *still* felt it.

He shook his head, willing it to dissipate. He was a brilliant surgeon at one of the nation's top hospitals. Why couldn't he work through his feelings for a woman he'd just met?

"So…you like her?"

"I did. I mean, I do." He exhaled a hiss of breath. "But we agreed it was only a one-night thing. She wanted to concentrate on her new job, and well, you know me."

"You want to concentrate on your job. Period."

"Yeah. Exactly." Brian and Mallory knew him best and loved him regardless of his work ethic, which others had dubbed *obsessive*. Aiodhán chose to think about it like a scientist: if a series of experiments all warranted the same negative results, the responsible thing would be to choose another course of action.

Life kept taking people he loved, so the answer was easy. Scientific. Clinical.

He simply didn't let anyone close to his heart.

"Bud, you're worrying me. Mind getting to the point so I know you're okay?"

"She's *here*." Aiodhán could feel her, even though half an ER separated them. She'd gotten too close that night. Her gaze had seemed to push through his walls. Worse still, he'd gotten the sense that, if he'd spent more time with her, she'd find the keys to the chains holding the walls up.

"Like, as in the hospital?"

"Yeah."

"Is she a patient?"

"Nope."

"A family member to someone you worked on?"

"Uh-uh."

There was a beat of silence on the other end.

"So she's…?"

"Yep."

"Damn."

Aiodhán nodded, even though his friend couldn't see him.

"That's an HR nightmare, isn't it?"

Aiodhán glanced at the pillow he'd taken his frustrations out on. He wanted to either kick it, scream into it, or lie down on it and restart the day—back to a time before knowing the woman he'd had trouble getting off his mind was one of his new interns.

"I hadn't thought about that."

"Well, I'd suggest you start. If I were you—and brother, let me tell you how glad I am that I'm not—I would swing by human resources and file a We Didn't Know We Worked Together form."

"They have those?" How often did this sort of thing happen?

"No, they don't have them, Ad. My God." Brian laughed, and Aiodhán's frown deepened. This wasn't funny. This was his career on the line. "Just go to HR and tell 'em what happened. You didn't know who she was, it won't happen again, blah, blah. And let me get back to my honeymoon, please. I've got a gorgeous blonde waiting on me with a mai tai, and neither are getting any happier that I'm out here with you."

"Sorry to bug you. Thanks for the advice, though."

"My pleasure. You've given me things to talk about between meals and bed."

"Please leave me out of your pillow talk. I've got enough problems. Anyway, see you when you're back. We'll go out for drinks, my treat."

"You bet."

Brian hung up, and Aiodhán inhaled, letting the cool air filter through his lungs, waking him up.

Time to get to work. Relationships he couldn't do, but run a new intern program? Yeah, he was built for that.

Ripping open the door to the hospital's locker room, he called inside. "Let's go. Time's up."

"Most of us are here, Dr. Adler," a confident, *accented* voice said from behind him.

He wheeled around and froze. Emilia had been stunningly beautiful the night he'd met her, in a deep green tank top that showed off her toned shoulders and breasts he'd enjoyed the rest of the night.

That was nothing compared to how she'd knocked him on his ass just now. *Again.* Her wild crimson curls were pulled back, accentuating the flawless, smooth curve of her neck, but one errant curl framed her forehead. He clenched his fists until he felt the flesh of his palms sting. Touching her, even to tuck the hair back, was forbidden on so many levels.

Of course Emilia would make the pale blue scrubs and lab coat she wore look like something off the catwalk. They managed to accentuate curves he hadn't forgotten in the past two weeks. Curves that kept him up at night, dreaming of how he might trace them with the tips of his fingers once more.

But she was his intern, his physician-in-training, his employee. So that couldn't happen. Not if he wanted to keep his job as chief of general surgery or practice medicine anywhere ever again.

Even if she wasn't any of those things, I can't have her. I can't have anyone.

Why did it feel as if he'd have to remind himself of that more than once over the next month?

He needed to talk to her, acknowledge what had happened and see where she was at with it. Maybe then, he could work in peace.

"Emilia, can I see you over here?" He gestured to an open space near the nurses' station where they wouldn't be overheard, but where he could protect both of their reputations by not hiding behind closed doors.

However, even in view of everyone, he could feel the way his body reacted to Emilia, to her soft, sweet scent and confident demeanor.

"Dr. Adler," she said.

"I wanted to apologize for not telling you fully who I was the other night. I've gotten a lot of interest from women who like me for my position here, and I liked talking to you anonymously."

Her gaze narrowed. "I understand that," she said. When she didn't elaborate, he continued.

"I understand if you can't work under me or need to report this to HR, but I assure you I'll remain professional from this moment forward."

Even if I feel like I'm being eviscerated every time I imagine your lips on mine.

"I'm fine. Thank you for your concern, but I can be professional, too."

She was fine, wasn't she? In fact, she didn't seem concerned in the slightest.

A twinge of something—frustration, maybe—tickled his skin. He didn't want her hurt, or pining after him, but a little bit of acknowledgment would have been nice. He rejoined the herd of interns, confusion sitting at the edge of his thoughts.

"All right. Well, let's start the tour, then. Take notes because I'm not going over this material again."

Aiodhán strode off, the interns filing in behind him like ducklings. At the nurses' station, Emilia was the only one who pulled out a pad of paper and pen, ready to note down what he taught. She was the only one taking him seriously.

He thought back to the bar. She'd been jostled by him but kept her chin and chest raised. And in his bedroom that night…

She'd been serious then, too, but in the goddamn best of ways. He shook his head, disrupting the image of her on top of him.

The intercom shot to life.

"Code Blue. Team needed in the ER."

"I meant what I said. Take notes," he said to the rest of them, already taking off down the hallway. "Looks like we're learning on the go today. Follow me." They fumbled, while Emilia strode beside him, her shoulders thrown back in the same way as they'd been at the bar. No hurt in her eyes.

Good. Maybe there was hope they could work together, then?

The ER was pandemonium. At least three gurneys were rolled in by EMTs, and more sirens whined in the distance.

"Give it to me," he said to the charge nurse, Mary. "What do we got?"

An EMT cut in. "Six-car collision on the I-35. One car almost went over. Three dead on scene, ten inbound in bad shape. These three are the worst."

Aiodhán whistled as he washed his hands in the scrub sink. "That damned bridge is cursed. Where do you need me? I'll have an audience, but put me to work."

"Why?" Emilia asked.

"Because you're here to learn," he shot back. This wasn't the time to challenge him. Confidence was fine, but he needed their respect as a teacher, too. Couldn't she see they were in the thick of it?

"Why is the bridge cursed?" she asked, donning a surgical gown and gloves as Mary handed them out. The rest of the residents looked perplexed, for which he couldn't say he blamed them. This was a helluva way to start their time at Minnie Gen.

But not Emilia. She looked ready to go. Was there any place she didn't seem in control?

"It collapsed almost twenty years ago. Thirteen fatalities and a hundred and forty-five casualties. Every bed in every hospital was full. C'mon."

"That's horrible," she whispered. It had been. Even now, he could still smell the burnt steel, hear the screams of the victims. It'd been…awful.

For him, especially. That was the day he'd become an orphan. It was also his first month of residency.

Both his parents were gone, both in accidents, but a decade apart. Neither had seen what he'd accomplished in his own residency. Heat built behind his eyes.

"We don't have time to worry about that. Let's get to work. De Reyes, you're with me. Everyone else, join us when you decide to get dressed."

He was too sharp, too short, but there wasn't room for his emotions or theirs. Only saving the patients mattered. Each life he saved added one to the scales against a universe that seemed hell-bent on taking from him for its own scale.

Emilia lifted the patients' eyelids and pulled out a penlight.

"Unresponsive. No pupil dilation. Should I call for a CT?"

"Okay. Order it. And de Reyes?" he said as she headed for the nurses' station. She nodded that he should continue. "Get those other residents in here, stat."

Dammit. Forget overexaggerating his feelings. This was gonna be impossible, wasn't it?

He needed to figure out how to work with a woman who had such a visceral effect on him. And who understood medicine on a cellular level. The only other Minnie Gen resident who'd ever been as unfazed in the ER in the midst of a crisis was himself.

Three hours later the team was exhausted. Only one resident had thrown up when they'd had to crack a chest cavity in the ER while they waited for a surgical room to open up. Three others had blanched but held it together. Maybe they wouldn't be the worst group he'd had.

Especially Emilia. She'd performed CPR for twenty minutes on one of the crash victims and hadn't missed a beat until they'd had to call TOD from brain death. She only nodded, called it, and walked out to change her gloves before moving to another room.

She was efficient as hell. And would make a damned good doctor, especially under Mal's tutelage. He struggled to find fault with her, and he needed something—anything—to get her off his mind.

He sent them all to the skills lab and made his way back to the nurses' station.

Aiodhán rethought Emilia's performance today. It meant the possibility of her earning chief resident if she kept it up. Working even closer with her was out of the question. He was already too distracted by the doctor.

But he'd never keep her from it, either. Which meant he needed to find some other way to distance himself from the woman.

A plan formed in his head, but it only covered the next twenty-four hours. Finish his shift, go for a long run along the river, then have enough whiskey to pretend the day hadn't happened. That Emilia de Reyes hadn't happened. It would work—hell, he'd done something similar when he'd realized he was alone in the world.

But it wouldn't last long, not with his liver intact.

And it had to. Not just for the next month, but for after that when his building—a world-class surgery and recovery center for victims of violence—was finished and he could start building a team to run it with him. It was all he'd wanted since he was eleven years old, and he'd be damned if anything pulled his focus. Even—*especially*—Emilia de Reyes.

But just saying it to himself didn't make it true.

Dammit. How the hell was he supposed to get through the next *two years* with this woman under his watch?

CHAPTER THREE

THE PERSISTENT BUZZING of her cell phone against her stomach made her cringe. She'd tucked it away in her lab coat pocket, silenced in anticipation of the work day ahead of her, but that didn't stop the outside world from encroaching on her.

"If you ignore them, Emilia, they'll only find other ways of reaching out. Ways you may not appreciate, *verdad*?"

"*Entiendo*. I understand." As crazy as Chance drove her with his helicoptering over her health and work, it was nice to hear snippets of her native tongue from time to time. "But they're going to have to wait. I have a busy day, and what they're calling about won't be fixed in the hundred meters to the front doors."

She stepped out of the car, waving him off. He got out anyway but stayed close to the driver's side.

"Don't you think they deserve to hear your progress?"

The thing was, she wanted to hear the only two voices who'd brought her any calm in the forest fire that had become her life. But what could she say?

I'm a disaster. I slept with my boss, I've barely eaten or slept since, and I'm thinking this was a mistake.

She couldn't let them down, not after her fiancé had thrown all their lives into a cyclone of grief and betrayal. The country was still reeling. *Emilia* was still reeling.

And she was *exhausted*. So much for healing and making this trip a restorative one.

"What progress? I'm two months into a two-year residency. I've got a long way to go, and they'll have to get used to not hearing from me every day. I barely have enough time to manage two meals a day."

"And if they ring me? What shall I say to them? Aside from the fact that their daughter is skipping meals."

Emilia rolled her eyes and pointed a finger at her guard.

"You won't mention my meals, thank you very much. Just tell them I'm fine, but busy, and that I'll call them over video chat on my next day off."

"And when might that be, Princess? Next year?"

"Shh…" Emilia glanced over her shoulder. Only the head of the hospital knew who she was and had assured her that her title would be kept quiet, as it had no bearing on her status at the hospital. Emilia was one of the first to arrive most days, something she was grateful for today, as the employee parking lot was empty. "You can't go shouting that word, Chance. But no, I'll be off shift this Monday. I'll call then."

"Sorry, Your Highness," he replied, dipping his chin. She shot him a scowl, but it didn't do much to deflect the smile on his lips. A jet-black SUV drove into the lot, and Emilia stood straighter.

"I've got to go, but please convince my folks I'm doing well."

"As you wish," Chance said, dipping into a low bow just as the familiar SUV parked three rows ahead of her. She rushed to catch up to it, hoping to deflect from Chance, who was still midbow.

"You are *such* an arse," she whispered under her breath at the man.

"Excuse me?" Aiodhán asked, materializing before her.

She gaped up at him, wishing for all the world she didn't have the palest, most translucent skin in the Mediterranean. Right now, she wagered her cheeks were a deep crimson.

"Sorry, I wasn't talking about you."

Aiodhán nodded, locking his G-Class with a click of a button. Emilia tried not to stare, but the way his Henley collar stood around a neck she'd kissed and his form-fitting jeans hugged thighs that had wrapped around her waist made it nearly impossible.

She'd really slept with her boss, hadn't she? Two and a half months wasn't even close to enough time to forget the evening with Aiodhán, nor was she sure she wanted to. But it would be nice if it didn't consume her every thought whilst she worked alongside the man.

He glanced over toward the edge of the parking lot where her gaze had traveled from.

"Who is that guy?" Aiodhán asked. "And why's he always hanging around till you get off?"

Emilia hadn't thought anyone noticed. Chance

was entirely chosen for his ability to fold into his surroundings.

"He's my roommate," she responded, her gaze locking with Aiodhán's. It was the party line she'd been told to spout if anyone asked, but it sounded trite. Who would believe a roommate would wait all day in the hospital parking lot so he'd be available when Emilia's shift was over? Not even a beau would be that dedicated. "He's using the hospital Wi-Fi to look for jobs in the parking lot. Says it's less expensive than finding a coffee shop."

"A roommate, huh? I guess that's better than the alternative."

The alternative? What might that be—a suitor? Aiodhán, who'd all but ignored her existence at the hospital except to bark orders at her, couldn't care about her dating life, could he?

Not that she had a dating life. Even if it *were* something she wanted, when would she find the time? No, she'd been married to her title and crown at home, and to the hospital here. It was fine. Real marriage would come all too soon. She somehow, even through her bone-weariness, thought she'd prefer this to sleeping beside someone other than Aiodhán. He'd set the bar rather high, hadn't he?

She would never show her distaste for whomever her parents chose, though. It was her duty, and she was proud to do what she was able for her country, for her family.

But, oh, would she carry her memories with her! Even small ones, like catching Aiodhán glancing at her when he thought she wasn't looking. And the small touches, their hands grazing each other when she passed him a scalpel, the way he'd accidentally brush by her in the hall, their shoulders touching.

Was she imagining their effects?

When Aiodhán strode over to the Lincoln Town Car, a stone of dread—always at the ready at the base of her throat since she'd left home—fell to her stomach.

"What are you doing?" she said, hurrying after him. She'd only been at Minneapolis General for eight weeks. Getting found out now would be terribly inconvenient.

But he ignored her. Of course.

When he got to the car, he rapped on the driver's window. Emilia shook her head behind him as Chance rolled down his window.

"May I help you, sir?" Chance asked, his accent thicker than hers. Would Aiodhán draw the obvious conclusion or make up one of his own? Which would be worse?

"I'm Aiodhán Adler, a surgeon here."

"A pleasure. My name is Chance. And how may I be of assistance to you?"

Aiodhán chuckled, shaking his head. "Um, I just wanted to invite you to use the Wi-Fi in the lobby. It's only gonna get colder out here the closer we get to the holidays. Plus, I don't want someone to call the cops on you for squatting in the parking lot."

"Pardon me? Squatting? The Wi-Fi?"

Aiodhán glanced back at Emilia, a question in his gaze, and she jumped in.

"Chance, what *my boss* is saying is that you're welcome to come sit in the lobby to use the internet for your job search."

Chance's eyebrows reached comic heights, and the corner of his lips twitched up into what she'd assume was a grin if Chance ever deigned to smile. Emilia held her breath.

"I see. Well, isn't that a kind offer? Though, I did think you told me not to come near the hospital entrance, Your—"

"Well, that was before Dr. Adler's kind offer, which I do *insist* you take."

Chance smirked. "Of course. I'll be in momentarily. I only need to finish this important call. About a *job* I was given to do."

Emilia's skin heated with a blend of frustration mixed with fear. Her lips clamped tight.

"Oh, you already found something?" Aiodhán asked. "Good for you. Well, nice to meet you, Chance. See you around. De Reyes, we should probably get inside."

"Of course." Emilia followed Aiodhán, awaiting his questions with bated breath.

"He's an interesting guy" was all that came.

Emilia breathed out a sigh of relief. "You have no idea."

"How'd you meet him?"

She decided on a version of the truth. "He worked

for my father, and I needed a roommate to be able to come to Minnesota for the program."

She felt Aiodhán's gaze on her, but she kept her eyes locked on the entrance to the ER. She couldn't get there fast enough.

"Why'd you pick Minnesota General? Your skills are already honed. You could have had your pick of programs."

Was that a compliment from her stoic, terse boss? "Thank you. But I needed someplace…quieter. I'm only here to learn what I don't know yet and be the best physician I can be."

Aiodhán stopped walking and gazed down at her. His eyes flashed with intensity, and his brows were pulled together in seriousness.

"What drives you, Emilia?"

She froze, her cells locking up one by one under his scrutiny and such an intimate question. And he'd used her first name.

"My mother." The rest of the words choked Emilia, thickening in her throat. Those two words had shifted meaning in the past few months, but the answer was the same.

"She's a doc as well?"

Emilia shook her head.

"She died when I was seven." She stood taller, pulled her shoulders back. There was no reason it should still hurt, not when it had been two decades. But there was a raw wound over an old scar now. Damn Luis for finding and pulling the thread that had led him to her mother's hospital records. Because the queen had been at the university down-town when her bleeding started, she'd been admitted there first. While she and Emilia's brother had died at home later, the evidence was there—the father on record was a member of the guard. The King's Guard.

When Aiodhán's hand rested on her shoulder, warmth flooded down from the spot he touched, radiating across her torso. Though it did nothing to tamper the hurt living wild in her chest, it awakened other parts of her that had been asleep her whole life, save the one night she'd spent with the doctor. "I'm sorry to hear that. Loss is a helluva powerful motivator. But—"

"Adler. Get in here. Got a trauma and no surgeon," a man called out from the entrance, interrupting Aiodhán. What was the *but* he'd referred to?

His hand lingered for a brief moment longer before his eyes hardened into the stone jewels they usually were.

"Let's go, de Reyes." He took off toward the entrance, and she followed at a run. "Dress out and meet me in Trauma One in two minutes."

As she donned her scrubs and coat alongside the night shift interns, she ran through the words he'd been prevented from saying. Had he gone through similar loss? Sometimes, when they worked a trauma as a team, he got this faraway look in his eyes. She imagined he was seeing something she couldn't, something from his past.

Not that he'd share anything personal with her. No, he was too professional. Surgically efficient.

When the beeping from Trauma One grew loud enough to hear from the hallway, she put aside any thoughts of Aiodhán and his odd behavior.

It was time to do what she came there to do, and under no circumstances was a man going to stand in her way.

CHAPTER FOUR

AIODHÁN TIGHTENED THE tie around his neck and gave himself a once-over in the mirror of the on-call bathroom. He looked professional. Competent. In charge.

Giving his watch a glance, he bit the corner of his lip. For the next few minutes anyway. Why was it every time he was in the orbit of Emilia de Reyes, all that went out the damned window?

He'd never once suffered a crisis of confidence at work—until the redheaded temptress entered his life. Now he second-guessed every last thing he'd been taught, said, even wore.

"Get a grip," he told his reflection. "You're the goddamn chief of general surgery. You can handle this." If the last eight weeks were any indication, however, that wasn't entirely true.

Emilia had been *brilliant* in the ER the morning before. Quick reflexes, she'd anticipated his requests, and her calm had been contagious. He'd worked through the GSW with an energy and serenity he'd never felt in the ER. She was the best intern to walk through the doors of Minny Gen. Himself included. He'd picked it up—the rhythm, the work ethic—after a few months, but Emilia came with it bred into her. Nothing seemed to faze her.

And he'd tested that theory.

Eight weeks of routine scut work, never-ending rounds that residents had to make, even the toughest patients with horrible attitudes… Other interns were burnt out, and she smiled through it. Hell, she even got some of the hard cases smiling, too.

"Three things, Adler," Mallory had told him when he agreed to take over the residency program. "Passion, responsibility, and professionalism. You find a resident with all three at the end of their first year, don't let them go."

"I'm not an idiot, Mal." Of course he'd hang on to the good ones.

"That may be true, but you are—how should I put this?—grumpy enough to put Scrooge on the Nice List."

He'd balked at the accusation, but now he wondered. Was he pushing and testing Emilia, or driving her away? He hoped not. Wasn't he always saying that the job mattered more than anything else? And she was good for the hospital.

It wouldn't be the worst thing if she found another program.

Yeah, it would, his head argued against the criticism of his heart. *She deserves to be here,* the balancing scales in his heart argued. She helped him save lives, which was his only goal.

She also made him forget all about that goal one evening when they'd been locked in the skills lab together during a tornado warning. She'd bet him she could assess and analyze more correct case studies and he'd shaken her hand, taking that bet with the overconfidence earned by his years on the job. That'd been his downfall. Her scent had overwhelmed him, and to compensate, he'd gotten over-confident and misdiagnosed three patients.

Fake patients, but still. De Reyes was killing him. No, his reaction to her was killing him. None of this was her fault, something that bugged him more than anything: she was doing just what he'd promised he would and kept things professional since day one.

He'd truly believed he could do the same thing. That he couldn't had to imply some sort of weakness he'd not addressed in himself yet.

The speaker overhead blared. "Dr. Adler to the nurses' station."

He needed to forget Emilia and focus on the trauma building across the street and start the interview process for docs to join him there. Thank God the residents moved to rotations next month.

"Dr. Adler to the nurses' station." The page sounded again and he jogged over.

"What do you have for me, Kathy?" he asked, grateful for work to distract him from thinking of Emilia. Again.

Always.

He swallowed that and concentrated on Kathy's rundown.

"Female patient, twenty-three years old, trouble breathing. Your intern is already in with her, taking vitals."

"Isn't that your job?"

Kathy just shrugged. "Wasn't my idea. She was halfway through when I got here. Doing a good job, so I figured I'd let her finish."

"She?"

"That new doc from Europe."

Damn.

"Okay," he said. "Thanks."

He grabbed a tablet and headed to the room Kathy indicated. The interns weren't even supposed to be on shift till now, and it looked like she'd been here at least half an hour.

But sure enough, before he even walked through the clear, glass doors to the patient's room, Emilia's laughter rang out.

The laugh was so incongruous with the space, it rubbed him the wrong way. No, that wasn't wholly the truth. If he were being honest with himself, he was frustrated because everyone else seemed to get this side of Emilia—the fun-loving, effervescent one. Everyone but him.

"What do you see, Dr. de Reyes?" he asked, pulling up the patient's chart.

The woman was young—too young for the indicated hypertension.

Emilia's smile fell. What was it about him that forced her to hide that beautiful smile of hers?

Maybe it's a good thing. It's distracting.

And it wasn't his job to make Emilia happy…

But you wouldn't mind it, his heart argued.

Maybe not. But making her happy would lead to caring about her, and caring led to—well, it led to all kinds of places Aiodhán avoided.

"I've made the notes in her chart, but it looks like hypertension and some resulting complications," she said. When the patient's brows pulled with concern, Emilia added, "Ms. Delaney and I were just discussing the new dating show while I changed her bedpan and took her vitals. You're looking good right now, Ms. Delaney."

The patient calmed, as did her rapid heart rate.

"If only my husband agreed. He said these gowns make patients look like Monty Python characters."

The two women laughed. Her laugh might be yet one more thing about her that distracted him, but Aiodhán certainly didn't mind the way Emilia's skin flushed when she smiled, like her whole body wanted in on the pleasure. That is, when it didn't remind him of the way her skin had flushed under his touch the night they'd met.

Had that really been two and a half months ago? Why could he still recall each cell on her cheeks as they changed color for him?

He shook the images from his mind. He needed to keep this professional. In this case, he couldn't find fault in her job, either: she'd done good work.

Go a little easier on her. If this were anyone else, you'd be kinder, more patient.

When she got out a saline bag, however, he stopped her.

"You need to wait for the other interns. And this is a nurse's job. You're a physician." He argued with himself that was a fact, something he'd tell any of the interns.

Emilia's brows furrowed, and she hung the bag without attaching the IV.

"But if I can do it, and I'm available, doesn't it make sense for me to help out?"

"It's a precedent we don't want to set. There's a reason we don't cross-train here."

Emilia opened her mouth as if she meant to shoot back a retort but shut it again, shaking her head.

"I feel nauseous again, Emilia," Ms. Delaney said. Her color had indeed changed to a pale gray. Emilia had a bedpan under her in seconds, just as the other interns finally rolled in. Aiodhán checked his watch. Ten minutes late. Emilia was the only intern pulling her weight, and then some.

The patient vomited into the bedpan as Emilia placed the IV for fluids without asking for permission. Emilia breathed through her mouth, her own skin dappled with moisture and nearing the color of her patient's. Aiodhán didn't miss the way a wave of nausea rolled through her.

"Are you okay?" Bridget asked her.

"Yes, thank you."

Aiodhán moved beside her. "If you can't handle bodily fluids, de Reyes—"

"I'm fine." Her skin paled even more than the translucent cream it usually was, but she kept going until the line was placed.

Aiodhán inspected her work, then shook his head. "It's not right. Try it again."

"Would you care to explain how? It's placed precisely where you indicated it should be."

Aiodhán took a moment to compose his response. She was right, on one hand. It wasn't that the line wasn't placed correctly, but it wasn't the way he'd have done it. And that's what mattered—consistency. Still, he had to admit she had an inherent skill the other interns were slow to come to. They were learning where she seemed to just…know.

"You've taped it incorrectly. On top of the arm allows for easier access to the port."

Warning prickled his skin when she scowled.

"This gives her more range of motion."

As if to prove her point, the patient vomited again, and the line didn't tangle or pull.

Thankfully, she didn't gloat about her win. Instead, she rubbed the patient's back, talking softly to her.

Hmmm. Good bedside manner, flexibility in patient care, top-notch skills… Mallory would be pleased. Why wasn't he?

Because you're afraid if she's too good, she'll get snapped up by another hospital after her residency. A more prestigious program.

That hadn't occurred to him until now. The only thing worse than having to work with Emilia for two years, all the while craving her in every sense of the word, would be to see someone else claim her.

He continued, his skin prickled with goose bumps. "Based on the medical history this patient shared, what's the next step in diagnostic reasoning?" he asked the room. The three other interns who'd arrived dove into the notebooks they'd taken to carrying with them since the first day, as if they might find the answer there.

Emilia's hand was the only one that rose confidently.

"Of course she knows," one of the interns mumbled under their breath. Another snickered.

"You two are jackasses," Bridget mumbled. Aiodhán bit back a smile. She was right on that count.

"If one of you has the answer, you're welcome to share it," Aiodhán told them. He might be frustrated by Emilia's natural proclivity for giving right answer after right answer if only because it meant he had to focus his attention on her, something he fought the urge to do day after day anyway. But for a lower-performing student to disparage her for it? Not on his watch. "Well, come on. Do you have anything?"

"I don't, Dr. Adler," the first said. When he trained his gaze on the man who'd laughed, the intern shook his head as well.

"Very well. What do you think, de Reyes?"

"Run an echo and electrocardiogram and have a full blood panel drawn."

"Looking for what, specifically?"

"Heart disease and a blockage that might explain the shortness of breath with the patient. Specific worry about a prestroke clot should also be watched over the next twenty-four hours."

He'd bet by the open mouths on the other interns' faces, their eyes wide with surprise, they were thinking of something lung-related. They'd have been wrong.

"Why is that?" he asked.

"The patient was on estrogen birth control until

this month when she tried to conceive. In addition to trouble breathing, she presented with a family history of clots and a mother who suffered a fatal stroke at around the patient's age."

Aiodhán nodded. Most others would have missed the history of clots and birth control. Especially their first two months on the job.

"Good work." Giving her praise was awkward: he felt as if the whole room could see through to his feelings for the resident. But they needed to see what competence looked like. That was the job. "So, what are you waiting for? Order the tests, and check in on the labs. Report back on the results as they come in. You've earned it."

Emilia nodded and spun on her heels, and like everything she did, there was an air of confidence in her step, in the way her shoulders remained tall and proud even under his scrutiny. She was thinner than when she'd arrived, likely the demanding schedule. Her skin was pale, too. She'd adjust, but his heart tugged. He'd been working her too hard.

He sent the interns on rounds, then ran to catch up with her. "Emilia, wait."

She turned to face him. "Yes, Dr. Adler?"

What did he want from her? Nothing he could ask for, nothing he should pursue for so many reasons. *Walk away.* And he almost did. Until his eyes caught the door to an on-call room. Her eyes flashed with something he recognized from their night together. Desire.

Before he could talk himself out of whatever it

was he was doing, he pulled her in and shut the door. Emilia's back was to the wall and her eyes were round as she gazed up at him. Her chest rose and fell with each breath she took through parted lips. He knew the curves of her breasts by heart, even after only one night of giving them all the pleasure he knew how to give. But they appeared fuller, heavier. Maybe that was just his imagination that knew no bounds when it came to Emilia de Reyes.

Goddamn, she was stunning. His hand reached up of its own volition and wrapped around the base of her ponytail before his brain could redirect him to less dangerous ground. His thumb traced her pronounced cheekbone. She inhaled a small gasp, and color spread to her cheeks. But she didn't move out of his grasp or try to move away from him. In fact, she leaned into his palm, closing her eyes as a soft smile played at the corner of her lips.

That—the smile he'd missed on her lips for so many weeks now—undid him.

"I'm just Aiodhán," he whispered. "Not your boss or even someone you work with. Just the man you met at the bar that night."

"You…you can't be that. Not anymore."

A whisper tickled the back of his mind.

She's right. What are you doing?

What he'd wanted to do for weeks now but couldn't. Touch her, which he did, trailing his thumb along her full, pink bottom lip.

"Please," he whispered. She nodded. He dipped

his chin and claimed her mouth, used his tongue to open her mouth so he could explore her.

She deepened the kiss by pulling him closer, and with her chest pressed against his, he didn't have any doubt—her breasts were swollen and fuller than they'd been. Goddamn. The desire ripped through him fast and hot until a Code Blue alarm sounded outside the door.

She shot back against the on-call bed, leaving him struggling to catch his breath.

Emilia's eyes grew even wider if it was possible, and her fingers traced her lips where his had just been.

"We can't do this. I—I'm not available, Aiodhán."

"You're with someone?"

She shook her head. "No. Not exactly. But I can't be with you. It wouldn't be fair." Those last four words came out as a whisper.

"I'm sorry," he got out through a ragged breath. "I don't know what came over me." He was her boss. Of course this wasn't fair to her. Jesus. What had he done?

If pretending he didn't want her was hard before, it was impossible with her taste on his lips. But he had to.

"I've got to get back." She opened the door just enough that the harsh fluorescent lights poured in through the crack, reminding him of what lay beyond the on-call room. Namely an unjust world where the one thing he thought he wanted most he couldn't have without risking everything he needed.

He left the small room, and the events of the past few minutes caught up to him.

What the actual hell did I do? Had he really just followed an intern on orders he'd given her, only to pull her into a room and kiss her within an inch of his life? Heat spread from his lips to his chest, then pooled low in his stomach. Yeah, that's exactly what he'd done.

Aiodhán shifted on his feet, tempted to follow her again to apologize, but how could he trust that's what he'd actually do when his real desire was evidenced in his lips that tingled with want, in his erection that wouldn't abate?

Getting a grip on both issues, he turned the opposite way that Emilia had gone and strode back to where the other interns were finishing up.

Damn if pulling away from that kiss was the hardest thing he'd ever done, after burying his parents. What had come over him? It wasn't that he didn't want her, but that had to come second to letting her grow as a surgeon or physician. Which led to another problem. If she was incredible at what she did, and as passionate about it as he was? Well, he'd have a hard time talking himself out of wanting her the way he did each time she smiled with those full lips of hers while she worked, each time her independence and confidence won over a patient or resident, each time she corrected a misdiagnosis. He already lost control, and they'd only been working together for a matter of months.

"Thanks for making sure they stayed on task,

Bridget," he told Emilia's friend, gathering the crew to finish the rounds. "As for the rest of you, it's time to learn what scut work is. You can go ahead and put those notepads away. You won't be needing them the rest of the shift."

When they all grumbled, doing what he asked at a glacial pace, he sent a glance to where Emilia had just turned the corner. An ache that only partially had to do with being surrounded by her lesser motivated, poorer substitutes filled his chest. He missed her, dammit. Her lips, her hands, her sharp wit. But mostly how she made him feel when she was around. And that wasn't going to work.

Not for so many reasons, least of which was her enigmatic pull on his heart. His new job, in addition to running the residency program and finishing up across the street, was finding reasons for distancing himself from Emilia.

More than just his career and dream project were on the line if he didn't. His heart was at risk, and he swore he'd never wager that again on a relationship. Not even for a woman as captivating as Emilia de Reyes.

CHAPTER FIVE

"CAN I GET you anything, Princess?" Chance called out from the next room.

Emilia shook her head, but that wouldn't suffice, would it? Not when he couldn't see her. But she didn't have the energy for much else.

"I'm okay, Chance. Thanks."

She sank into the couch at her new apartment, letting the soft leather act as a balm for all that ailed her. Her toes curled against the sharp pain emanating from the arches of both feet. Her back cracked in two places, providing little relief to the pressure built around her spine. And why—*why*—did she have to pee again?

Honestly, it was as if every organ and muscle in her body joined in mutiny against her singular dream to practice the kind of medicine that would have saved her mother. Not that she blamed her body for putting up a fight. Even her heart was weary, not entirely sure *this*—the sixteen-hour days, the painstaking work of putting into practice all she'd learned in medical school, the loss of patients she'd grown to care for—was worth it.

She'd thought she was made of tougher stuff than simply princess material. But maybe she'd been wrong.

Then there was the persistent *thump-thump* of her heart every time she had to interact with Aiodhán.

From time to time she'd catch him staring at her, as if trying to figure her out.

It had only grown worse after their kiss. She put a finger to her lips and swore they still bore the heat that had passed between her and Aiodhán in that on-call room, even though it had been a month and he'd barely looked at her since.

She didn't blame him. She'd made it seem as if it would be unfair to her if they pursued a relationship. Even a physical one. But it'd been a lie, one meant to protect her cover. The truth was, she wanted him so desperately, she dreamed of his lips, his hands, his tongue…

But it would be so dreadfully unfair to him to let him in when the truth was she couldn't date, couldn't fall in love, couldn't have anything resembling a romance outside of her impending royal union.

That didn't stop the part of her that flushed with desire when she watched him work, when a hint of a smile graced his lips when he talked to a patient, or as he strode down the corridors of Minnie Gen. She still wanted him, whether or not she should.

And make no mistake, she *shouldn't*. In the past month since the kiss, she'd made sure to focus on work and work only. But in doing so, she'd become undernourished and overworked, with no time for the self-care needed to get back to full strength. Emilia picked up a pale green throw pillow that reminded her of the color of the Mediterranean Sea outside her family home and screamed into it.

It wasn't bad, but it wasn't *her*. She was a doctor.

A chime alerted her to the private elevator making its way to her penthouse.

Chance peered out from the kitchen, an apron tied around his waist.

"That's quite a look for you, Chance," Emilia said. A giggle escaped, earning her a frown from the uberserious adviser.

"Are you expecting company?" he asked, ignoring her quip about his attire.

"Relax. It's just a woman from my program. We're going to study and work on sutures together this evening."

"Do you think it wise to invite people here? Others knowing where you live puts you at risk, Princess."

"Well, luckily, that's what I have you for." Chance's scowl deepened if that was possible. "Please don't call me Princess while she's here, okay? It's just Emilia. Who cares where I live? If people find out who I am, *that's* when I'll be in trouble."

Chance didn't respond but went to the elevator doors that were opening on Bridget, typing something frantically on her phone.

"Okay, please explain why I needed a code to get in here—" She cut herself off as her gaze lifted. Her mouth dropped in surprise, and her long whistle echoed off the vaulted ceiling. "Holy crap. You live *here*? Why the hell are you an intern if you can afford to live like this?"

"May I take your coat?" Chance asked.

Bridget hugged her red pea coat close to her chest.

"Who is this?" she asked Emilia, jabbing a thumb in the direction of a wounded-looking Chance. Emilia sent the man a stare that hopefully expressed he was on thin ice. A roll of his eyes and quick turn on his heels and he was back in the kitchen.

"Never mind him. He's my roommate and comes from money."

It was a weak alibi, but when Chance reappeared with crudités on a tray, Bridget didn't question it.

"Oh, my *gawd*. We're never meeting at the library again. You've been holding out on me," she said, stuffing a salmon pâté cracker in her mouth. Emilia stifled a laugh. If life were any different, she'd love to take Bridget to see her home country. This penthouse was nice, but it paled in comparison to her coastal home in the south, or the castle in Cyana. Bridget would love it.

A small yearning to see it for herself nudged at Emilia's heart. She missed Zephyranthes, but this trip was important. She'd be back soon enough.

"I'm okay with that. Any luck on the moonlighting position?" she asked, grabbing a snack for herself. She had to give the guy credit: for all Chance's grumblings, he was a fabulous cook.

"Nothing yet. Aiodhán doesn't think I'm ready for the extra shifts here, so I started putting out feelers at hospitals outside the city."

Emilia bristled at the mention of Aiodhán. He took up so much space in her thoughts and life, but having his name spoken here filled the spacious room with an oppressively thick air.

"Yikes. Do you really need the extra work? I mean, we're barely off enough to sleep and get a meal on the run as it is."

Bridget shrugged. "I wish I could, but this city is expensive, and residency doesn't pay enough to cover rent."

Emilia curled up on the couch, her legs tucked beneath her. Other residents had expressed similar sentiments. This life—when one didn't come from her resources or wealth—wasn't for the weak of heart.

Was there something she could do to help, or would that come off as patronizing?

"I'm sorry," she said, but it sounded weak, especially since they were surrounded by Zephyr art and decor that cost enough she could have housed the whole residency for cheaper.

"It's fine. Not all of us are as lucky as you, finding your way into this life. You're like Minneapolis royalty up here."

A slow burn traced Emilia's skin, painting it red with embarrassment. She'd grown up around privilege and pomp and ceremony. Was she missing out by not adapting fully to life here? The truth was, she didn't know if she'd make it in the grueling residency program without Chance cooking for her and these comforts to come home to. As it was, she was barely able to stand.

"Well, my place is your place. You're welcome here anytime."

Two hours, three different appetizers, and one delicious chocolate mousse pie later, the women put aside their oranges and thread so Emilia could say good-night to Bridget. The poor fruit looked like something out of a horror film, with crude sutures stitched across their skins. But there was noticeable improvement.

A wave of pride washed over her own skin. Who cared what Aiodhán thought? She was good at this and, more importantly, she was willing to work and learn how to be better.

She stood up, prepared to head to her bedroom for the five hours of sleep she'd get if she fell asleep immediately but was rocked by a crippling wave of nausea.

Desperation to make it to the sink warred with her body's inability to move without a new crest of dizziness crashing against her. Immobilized, she vomited into the bowl still half full of gourmet popcorn.

"Chance?" she whispered. Somehow, the man heard her and was by her side in less than a breath's time. "I'm not well."

"No, you're not. You're pale, *Princesa*." He swept her up and before she could process what was happening, she was being tucked into her four-poster bed. She nestled between the down comforter and the pillowtop mattress, sleep claiming her as a final thought floated to her consciousness.

It's probably something you ate. You'll be fine in the morning.

With that, she fell into the deepest sleep since her arrival in America.

The next morning, feeling weak, Emilia sought out Bridget in the staff locker room.

"Are you feeling okay?" she asked her friend.

Bridget shot her a surprised look from under furrowed brows while she donned her lab coat labeling her a resident of Minneapolis General.

"Um, yeah. Why? Should I not be?"

Emilia shook her head, but the headache that had plagued her all night still pulsed behind her eyes.

"Of course not. I just felt...*off* last night and wanted to make sure it wasn't the salmon."

"Don't you dare blame that dish your roommate made. That was the best meal I've had in years." Emilia laughed, relieved. Her friend was okay. But if it wasn't the fish, what made her so ill so suddenly? "You're probably just exhausted."

"Yeah, you're probably right."

Bridget set down her stethoscope and appraised her closely. "You feel okay now? Because I'll vouch for you with Aiodhán if you need to take off today."

Emilia's stomach flipped.

"No, no. I'll be okay. I just want to get the day over with. Then I'm going home and going straight to bed."

The door to the locker room slammed open, crashing into the wall behind it.

"Let's go. You two are holding up the group."

Aiodhán. He hadn't heard anything they'd discussed, had he? If he had, especially after the week she'd had under his watchful eye in the OR, she'd never recover her reputation with him.

Why do I care so much what this man thinks?

Emilia's stomach flipped. Was it another side effect of whatever had upset her rhythm the night before? Perhaps she had a stomach bug that was a result of more than just dehydration and malnutrition. She tended to sick people all day, after all.

It didn't matter either way. She needed to get to work before Aiodhán found another excuse to be peeved with her.

As she stepped out into the light—far brighter than normal, wasn't it?—she swallowed back the pervasive nausea. Nothing was getting in the way of her dream that was so close she could touch it. Not even a little bout of stomach issues that would surely resolve in a matter of days.

CHAPTER SIX

Two WEEKS LATER, Aiodhán was actually worried. Emilia hadn't missed a shift or even been late once. But she wasn't herself either.

Outside the OR that morning, he'd been telling the intern class about fistulas and how to repair them, and her eyes had glazed over; she focused on the wall behind him and not the medical advice he was sharing. At one point, she sighed heavily and struggled to keep her eyes open.

Definitely not typical Emilia.

Then he'd offered the chance to scrub in to the first intern who could correctly name the four types of fistulas that might occur. The three residents all shot an expectant look at Emilia, as did he. After all, she was always the first to answer—correctly, too—when he posed a question to the cohort.

But nothing. Just another sigh capped with a yawn.

Definitely not typical Emilia.

"May I speak with you in the hall, de Reyes?"

She seemed to snap out of the stupor she was in and nodded.

"What's going on?" Aiodhán asked when they were alone.

"What do you mean?" The genuine look of surprise in her twisted brows and pursed lips didn't sit

KRISTINE LYNN   73

well with him. If anything, the woman was painfully self-aware. "Am I in trouble?"

"No." He shook his head, regret pulsing in his chest. He'd pushed her too far, and she blamed herself. "I'm sorry if I made you think you were."

"Then, I'm confused. Why are you pulling me aside? Did I miss a report?"

"No, nothing like that. You just seem…off. I asked about the four types of fistulas, and you didn't even glance over."

She frowned. "Anorectal, anovaginal, colorectal, and colocutaneous."

"Right." Of course she knew; he expected no less from her.

She'd be perfect for the trauma center. I want to take a resident or two, so why not her?

"So," he continued, "as you know I'll be moving my practice across the street."

"To the Minneapolis General Trauma Facility?"

"Yep. I was wondering if you'd be willing to do an extended rotation there. I need a good resident, and you're the best."

Emilia's lips parted like she might answer when a Code Blue alarm went off. Aiodhán's gaze shot to Kathy at the nurses' station.

"Trauma Three," she shouted over the din and chaos of the ER.

He nodded and glanced down at Emilia. "Join me?"

Her forehead raised in question. Aiodhán had never asked her for anything before today, had he?

Just demanded. Well, that would change. It had to if he didn't want to lose Emilia. As a doctor, of course. He didn't have any personal feelings toward the woman.

Liar, his libido chimed in. *You'd take her back to an on-call room in a second if you thought you wouldn't lose credibility or your job.*

Damn. That was true, but inconsequential. She'd shut him down, and thank goodness. If he still wanted her, it was his problem—not hers.

"Um…sure. For this case. May I take some time to consider the other offer? My heart is set on obstetrics as a specialty, but I'd like to weigh my options."

"Of course. You should know we'll have an OB wing there for trauma cases involving pregnant women. But take all the time you need to consider the offer," he said. Aiodhán lingered a fraction of a second, only then noticing her red-rimmed eyes. "You sure you're okay to do this?" he asked.

"I am."

He saw what it cost her to throw her shoulders back and lift her chin. *That* was typical Emilia. She'd be fine with some rest and time off. He'd make sure she got both next week. No matter how he acted in person, whatever front he put on for show, he cared about Emilia. Seeing her like this was like a mirror to all his mistakes being held up in front of him.

He gestured toward Trauma Three and jogged over, Emilia close on his heels.

"What's the story?" he asked Rana, the nurse on call. She was up on the bed performing CPR, but the steady beep rang in the background, indicating no sinus rhythm.

"GSW to the right flank, no exit wound. Waiting on a surgery room to open up. Coded thirty seconds ago. No pulse."

"Another one," Emilia whispered, shuddering. She wasn't wrong. There'd been an increase in gunshot wounds the past week. He could triage those cases easier than he could the car-wreck victims, though. The latter came too close to home for him.

"Come on down and push two of epi."

Emilia was already charging the paddles to two hundred, anticipating his ask.

"Okay, we only get one shot at this. I want to get him back, then open him up."

"Here?" Rana asked.

"Do we have another option?"

She shook her head, putting the meds in the IV. "Not for at least an hour."

"This guy doesn't have that long."

"I'll call and get the team here, along with a portable surgery tray," Emilia said. Before he could comment on the sterile field he'd need to make, she added, "But I'll have them wait behind the glass divider so you can keep a sterile field."

"Go for it, but hurry back. I need you to assist." It was the closest he could get to what he wanted to say. *Thanks for anticipating what I'll need and being a helluva partner in the OR.*

Within ten seconds, the other interns flooded the room on the back side of the divider so they could observe but stay out of the way, and Emilia rolled in a tray. The patient had sinus rhythm back, so if he was going to do this—open up a patient in the middle of the ER—he needed to do it now.

"Iodine," he said as he grabbed the scalpel he needed, but Emilia already had it in hand and was dousing the patient's abdomen. "Thank you. I want a portable ultrasound brought up and a recovery room booked."

"It's already on its way," Emilia said. "And the room is reserved. It was the last one available, and I didn't want us to lose it."

Damn it. She really was magnificent. In so many ways…

"Okay, then. Let's do this."

Emilia adjusted the light, and Aiodhán stilled before he cut. Her skin was pale and dappled with sweat.

"You sure you're up for this? You can observe if you'd like."

"No," she said, swallowing hard. "I'm okay. How can you use me?"

"Suction, and watch the ultrasound for shards of metal or the bullet. Best case we find it intact, but I'm not betting the farm."

"The farm?"

He chuckled, as did Rana. Using the scalpel, he sliced a ten-inch opening for them. "It's an American English expression meaning I don't think we will. Do you have an idiom like that in Spain?"

"I'm from Zephyranthes, actually."

"Oh." She hadn't so much lied to him as allowed him to make assumptions. But why not share where she was from in the first place? It didn't make a difference to him. "So, any Zephyr idioms?"

Emilia's smile brightened the room more than the overhead surgical light. She suctioned, her eyes on the wound, and her hands moved fluidly like she'd been doing this for years, not months. "The closest I can think of is an old one. *El tapete le acabó con cuanto poseía.* It means *The man lost his fortune at the gambling table.*"

"I like it. It's a helluva lot classier than ours. Suction."

Emilia moved the suction to the bleed Aiodhán found. She breathed through her mouth, slow and deliberate.

"Zephyr idioms always seemed more like life lessons when I was growing up. Do this and lose your and your family's good name. Say that and drown in sorrow for eternity."

"Damn. Well, with one of the few countries left with royalty running the show, that checks out."

"What do you mean?" she asked. A hint of color flushed her cheeks, but he couldn't focus on that now. Nor what it did to the fluttering in his stomach.

"Nothing, really. Just seems like all those staunch royals make things more serious than they have to be. I saw the king on the news the other day, and he had way too many medals on his chest for a guy signing in a new law. Suction, please." She moved the hose to where Aiodhán worked. "Thanks."

"Maybe we should stick to talking about medicine and not something we know so little about," she said.

He moved the lower intestinal tract out of the way and still…nothing. Was Emilia really passionate about all that pomp and circumstance? "Found it." Relief washed over him. His patient was deteriorating fast. All he could hope for now was a clean bullet and no internal bleeding. Emilia handed him a set of curved hemostat forceps without taking her gaze off him. He retrieved the bullet in one piece, no signs of fragmentation present. "Looks whole."

"I guess you didn't lose your fortune," Rana said, an overly wide smile on her face. The nurse was only trying to lighten the mood, but as Emilia sutured the patient up, her scowl didn't budge.

What the hell had he said?

After closing, Emilia cut the thread and put the scissors down on the tray. "If you don't need me for anything else." She moved in the direction of the door.

"Emilia," Aiodhán said. He kept his voice level, even though an undercurrent of so many emotions ran below it. "Can we talk?"

She shook her head, her back to him so he didn't see her face as her shoulders slumped. What happened next was both in slow motion and at the same time too fast for Aiodhán to react. Emilia's legs gave out, and she bent over her stomach before crumpling to the ground. Though his arms were outstretched, desperation driving him toward her, he was too late.

Emilia's body bounced off the gurney, and her head hit the tile floor with a sickening thwack that reverberated in Aiodhán's chest.

As time sped forward again, he sprinted to her side, only one thought on his mind.

Oh, God. Please let her be okay.

"Everyone out. I need a gurney *now*," Aiodhán said. Emilia was unconscious but breathing. He'd done a quick workup, and there didn't appear to be any damage to her neck and spine. But her pulse was thready, and she looked like hell.

He cupped her head, keeping it stable in case he'd missed something, and despite the optics of the situation he stroked the hair off her damp forehead with the pads of his thumbs. He shivered, a dark memory of holding his father's head in his lap playing at the edge of his consciousness. He couldn't help then, but he'd be damned if he let Emilia suffer the same fate as his old man.

"Why isn't anyone moving? Get her help *right goddamn now!*"

So much was at stake, and they were deer in the headlights.

"I'll grab the gurney," Bridget said.

"Wait. Do you know her roommate?"

"The rich Zephyr guy with the fancy apartment? Yeah, why?"

Aiodhán frowned. That was a lot of information he hadn't been aware of.

Not the time.

"Sure. Yeah. He's in the lobby. Sprint down and grab him in case he knows how to contact her family."

"You got it, boss." Bridget sped off down the hall, and the rest of the room cleared out, the steady beep of the gunshot patient's heart rate monitor peppering the silence until he was moved to his recovery room.

"I've never met anyone like you, Emilia. You make me—hell, you make all of us—so much better."

The admission surprised him. It was all true, but he'd always been able to shove aside his feelings, his memories—anything that might get in the way of his job. Until Emilia. She blurred lines he'd thought were etched in steel.

The door hissed open, and a nurse rolled a gurney through.

"Do you want me to help you get her up?"

"No," he said, shaking his head, his gaze still pinned on Emilia's unconscious form. A proprietary sense of ownership washed over him. He couldn't relinquish her care to anyone else. "I've got it, thanks."

He tucked an arm under her legs and stood, cradling her neck. She was light but limp in his arms, and seeing her without her signature strength and sass bit the back of his throat, making it hard to swallow. She didn't stir as he set her down on the gurney.

"Make a room available in the west wing," he told the nurse. "I'll take her up myself. But let her roommate and Bridget know where we're sending her."

She tapped a few things on her tablet and left.

"I've got you, Emilia. I won't let anything happen to you."

He made a mental list on the elevator to the west wing of what he'd need to take care of Emilia. Basic labs to see how malnourished she was, an IV of fluids, a CT to check her head for a concussion.

And what she needed? A few days off and for him to finally let her hold on him go. Maybe if their shared night of passion wasn't so prevalent in his thoughts, he'd have recognized she was sick.

He'd be better. For her, because she deserved a teacher who could live up to the same level of professionalism she showed up with every day.

If she makes it, his brain chose that moment to chime in.

She will. She has to. She's just a little overworked, right?

But small memories perked up in the back of his head. Her puking a few weeks earlier after a patient was sick. Overhearing her tell Bridget she was sick before that. This had been going on for a while, but he'd been too stubborn, too hurt by her dismissal of him, too rigid in his attempts to keep her at arm's length that he'd failed to act on what he'd seen.

The doors to the elevator opened, and Chance was standing there, a grim look on his formerly stoic face.

"Where, may I ask, are you taking Emilia? And what happened to her?"

"She passed out in the ER. I'm taking her to a

room so I can get a workup done. She hit her head pretty hard, so there are some tests I have to run."

"I'd like to see all the results."

Aiodhán maneuvered around Chance, realizing for the first time the girth of the man. With his arms crossed over his chest, he looked strong—strong enough to feel like he could demand the impossible.

"I'm afraid I can't do that. Family only. I appreciate your concern for Emilia's health, but—"

Chance slapped a folded sheet of paper against Aiodhán's chest as he walked by.

Okay, so the man didn't just *look* strong. Aiodhán coughed some air back in his lungs.

"This is her medical power of attorney, granting me access to her care, the decisions that need to be made on her behalf, and full rights to information until such time as her parents can be dispatched."

Until such time as *what*? Any other time, this guy's attitude and odd speech patterns would rub Aiodhán the wrong way, but right now? With Emilia's health on the line? It straight pissed him off.

"We're wasting time. Get out of my way before I call security."

Chance smiled in a way that sent a chill through Aiodhán's veins. It was less a grin and more a sneer.

"Do you think they'd like to learn you slept with Emilia the night you took her home to your apartment?"

Aiodhán stopped pushing the gurney and felt his jaw drop as his limbs froze.

"She told you?"

Chance shook his head. "She didn't need to. I make it a point to know everything Emilia is up to."

Aiodhán's finger was up in Chance's face before he could stop himself. The woman at the heart of the rage that boiled in his chest was lying unconscious beneath the men arguing over her care. Not okay. Not one bit.

"Now, listen here, you creep. If you don't move out of my way, I'll have you arrested for obstruction of care. Either way, I'm deciding whether to turn you in as a stalker. Call her parents, and stay the hell away."

His grip on the gurney tightened until his joints ached and his breath came in short bursts. That guy was a piece of work.

The room was set up already, Bridget hanging the last of the IV bags.

"Thanks," he told her. "I appreciate you working ahead of me. Can you order a set of bloodwork and labs? And schedule a CT. I want these yesterday, Bridget, with the results for my eyes only, okay?"

"Of course. I understand." Bridget's brows were marked with concern. "But, um, I thought you should know she threw up this morning and last night and wasn't feeling well."

A flash of anger singed Aiodhán's skin. Not at Emilia, for coming to work under the weather, but at himself for making her feel she had no other choice.

"I appreciate you letting me know. I'll swab her for the flu and run a couple other tests."

At the door, Bridget stopped and turned around.

"She's gonna be okay, right? She's the only person willing to talk to me here and who studies with me after our shift. Emilia is my best friend and the best of all of us."

Aiodhán couldn't agree more with the latter. If only he'd let down his guard with her and appreciated more of what she gave to the hospital, to her fellow interns who were studying and thriving so they might have a chance at keeping up with her, to *him*.

"I'm not sure what's going on, but I can promise I'll take good care of her."

Bridget smiled and left, but the door didn't close. Aiodhán looked up and frowned.

"I told you, man, get out of here now or I'll—"

Chance held up a badge, stopping Aiodhán in his tracks for the third time in as many minutes.

"I'll be staying, thank you," Chance said. Where the man had been humorously unsure of himself in the lobby, since he'd come up to the west wing, he exuded a presence that sent a chill across Aiodhán's skin. "I need to handle the secrecy of this until Emilia's parents arrive. It's imperative we contact them in a way that doesn't alert the wrong people to her…condition."

"And who would those people be?"

"Sir, I trust you're good at your job, am I correct?"

"Yeah. You could say that."

Chance dipped his head, as if in agreement. It was his first deference to Aiodhán's status.

"And I'm *superb* at mine, which is why I was chosen to travel with Ms. de Reyes. Please lock down any access to these quarters until I've given the green light. If you check with your CMO, you'll see she is already aware of the protocols."

Aiodhán's brows were arched, his curiosity piqued, but Chance didn't leave room for misinterpreting his commands. Aiodhán might have been in charge of his hospital, but Chance was in command of this situation: that much was clear now.

"Okay. I'll check back in once I've alerted the nursing staff and Bridget not to say anything."

"That won't be sufficient. I'll have NDAs distributed immediately. I need a list of names of people who are aware of Ms. de Reyes's stay here."

"Sure. Yeah. I can do that." *Why?* he wondered but wouldn't ask. He wasn't clear about *how* exactly, but this was bigger than him.

Aiodhán's arms fell to his sides, a feeling of inadequacy plaguing him for the first time since he'd first declared he'd wanted to be a doctor at the age of eleven. He'd stood there in nothing but plain white underwear, a stethoscope around his neck like his dad had worn.

"I'm gonna save people like Dad," he'd told his mom.

She'd been so supportive of that dream, even as a grieving wife who'd lost her husband to a car crash, doctors unable to save him. When his mother passed away in the horrific I-35 crash, leaving Aiodhán an orphan, it had solidified two things: he'd be the surgeon he wished he'd been to help save his parents, and he'd never let anyone else into his heart, which was a recipe for heartbreak.

And yet… Here he was, this woman very much infecting his heart. To what degree he'd parse through later, when she was okay. But damn if she'd somehow snuck past each of his carefully constructed defenses.

"May I ask you a question?" Aiodhán said to Chance, who nodded. "Why'd you need to travel with her? Why couldn't she do this alone?"

Thick, heavy silence filled the room with an edge of foreboding as Chance folded his arms across his chest again and nodded at Emilia on the bed.

"Because she's the crown princess of Zephyranthes, and my only job as royal adviser is to keep her safe."

CHAPTER SEVEN

"THE CROWN PRINCESS OF ZEPHYRANTHES? Like…a *real* Mediterranean princess?" Aiodhán asked. The room took on an eerie glow along the edges of his vision, and damn if pulling a breath was like sucking through a straw. His intern was a goddamned *royal*?

And part of the royal family he'd just unintentionally insulted while they operated a mere hour ago? No wonder she looked at him like he was the plague just before she… He shook his head, begging the image of her slumping to the ground, lifeless and pale, to dissipate. He doubted it ever would, though.

"Your knowledge of geography does your country justice," Chance retorted. The quirk of his lips said otherwise.

"And there are a lot of them? Royals? You know, like, for show? Dukes and princesses and whatever?" Why couldn't he recall what the news story had said? He was a bumbling idiot, trying to keep his head above water.

Chance's smile turned to one of pity.

"No, sir. Just the one. And her parents. The king and queen of Zephyranthes."

Aiodhán's thin field of vision contracted even further as heavier truths settled on his chest. First, there were actually *royals* out there, walking among the mere mortals instead of just on television. Hell, not even Minnesota was immune. But even bigger? Emilia, the incredible woman who'd infected his brain with thoughts of ridiculous, career-ending things like lust and passion, was one of them. And he'd hooked up with her in a night he wasn't likely to forget.

Oh, damn... His brain stalled as it struggled to process the reality of that simple discovery and exactly with it meant.

I slept with the princess of Zephyranthes. And then kissed her, breaking every international-relations rule that existed.

But wait... He wouldn't have kissed her if he'd known who she was. Indignation rolled through him, hot and fierce.

"She's a princess, and no one thought to tell me?"

"Was there a reason she should have disclosed that?" Chance asked. "Would you have treated her any different?"

"I mean, *yeah*."

Chance's smile grew thin. "Do you think, perhaps, that the choices you made would have been questionable whether or not Emilia was of royal lineage?"

Aiodhán sighed and put his head in his hands. "Damn. I'm sorry." He'd messed up, not just with the princess but the woman behind the crown. She deserved better no matter what title she bore.

"You might save that apology for the princess when she wakes up. And her parents might deserve an explanation as well."

"Yeah. Of course." Nerves fluttered in Aiodhán's chest. "And they're…"

"On their way here, yes. I'm sure they'll be delighted to meet Emilia's…" Chance paused, giving Aiodhán a head-to-toe assessment. *One-night stand,* Aiodhán filled in for him. "Boss," Chance ended with, mercifully.

Aiodhán paced the cold white-tiled floor while his brain raced with myriad thoughts about this new information.

Emilia was the princess of Zephyranthes.

Like a crown-wearing, title-bearing *royal*. He laughed.

"Is something funny?" Chance asked.

Aiodhán shook his head. "Tragic, actually. I mean, if I had been paying attention, I probably could have figured it out. Her confidence, the way she can talk to anyone and make them feel like they're the most important person in the room. All of it."

"The princess is regal, through and through."

And Aiodhán had done his damnedest to work that exceptionality out of her. And all because he couldn't get the captivating woman out of his head—or other parts of his anatomy. Looking too close at how she was struggling meant looking too close, period.

He was a royal, too. A royal *ass.*

Well, she's definitely unattainable now.

Another laugh escaped his chest. To anyone but Chance, he probably looked like he was losing it, and to a degree he was. Everything as he knew it was…different now. Who she was—a princess, yes, but also a fantastic doctor—was lined with a thousand red flags telling him to back off.

But damn if not one of those flags took the edge off the pulsing desire the woman brought out in him. Not even her lifeless form tucked beneath wires and hospital blankets did that; all it did was add a layer of protectiveness to the wanting.

Too bad both were misplaced. She had Chance for the latter, and protocols against dating a commoner—an American commoner—no doubt.

"Why couldn't I know?" he asked. "I mean, I wasn't just her boss."

"Precisely. We couldn't take the risk. There was a man who took advantage of her—of the entire family, actually—so anyone outside the upper echelon of administration knowing was too great a risk. Especially someone as…involved with the princess as you were."

"I'd never hurt her."

"I don't believe you would, not intentionally."

The idea of Emilia with another man was hard enough to imagine—but one who'd take advantage of her kindness, her intelligence for his own gain? Good thing there was an ocean between them. Still, it begged a particular question.

"Is she…" Aiodhán asked, peeking out of the curtains to make sure there weren't any lurking interns outside the door, eavesdropping. "Is she supposed to be with someone back home?"

Chance regarded him from under bushy brows.

"You care about her?" he asked Aiodhán.

Though the answer came to him immediately, he let it sit for a moment so he could choose his words wisely.

"I do. I know I'm not supposed to, especially with this new information, but…"

"She's special."

"She *is*. In so many ways." The way she understood what he needed—what their patients needed—without nudging, the way she anticipated questions and answered them in advance. But mostly the way she smiled no matter how tired she was. All the medical stuff could be trained into someone bright enough to pick it up. Yet her bedside manner? That couldn't be taught, and it was more than special: it was rare and beautiful. "But she'll have to marry someone back home, right?"

Chance's subtle nod might as well have been a hurricane-force wind the way it bowled Aiodhán over.

"It's part of her duty to her country, to make a union that will strengthen international ties. Her parents will make sure it's a proper match. Especially after the last attempt failed so grievously."

"The hell?" Aiodhán asked. His pulse was tachycardic, and his fervent pacing along the edge of her bed matched the speed of his racing heart. A primal scream welled up in his throat, suffocating him, but he didn't dare let it out.

"Where your geography does you proud, your lexicon falls short, Dr. Adler."

Aiodhán glared at Chance and jabbed a finger at the hospital bed.

"You're telling me this brilliant woman, the top of her class at one of the best teaching hospitals in the country, with passion that actually matches her skill…you're telling me she's betrothed to a guy she's never met? And after being screwed over by the last guy? Did I miss the train taking us back to the Dark Ages?"

"While I don't expect you to understand royal protocols—"

"Oh, don't give me that, Chance. You know as good as I do that the woman lying in that bed is way more than a crown or somebody's arm candy. She's a damn fine doctor, and she'll be squandered if she goes back there."

A flash of something resembling understanding passed over Chance's stoic features but passed as quickly.

"Emilia is aware of her obligations and takes them seriously. And she was always going to leave at the end of her residency. A two-year passion project is all our nobility are afforded, I'm afraid. Though her health might predicate her early exit from the program."

All this time, he'd made choices about her related to *his* needs and responses to the night they'd shared. He'd worried Emilia would stay and be a constant source of temptation for *him* or leave for another hospital and leave *him* wanting. The third option hadn't occurred to him. She wasn't even going to stay in this country because the woman owed *him* nothing. She'd shared a night of passion with him he'd never forget, but they'd never once talked about more.

He was losing her, no matter what. Which meant the hospital was, too. Faced with that possibility, he knew what was best for everyone. She needed to stay, to pursue medicine as long as she was able, and he needed to get the hell out of her way.

Aiodhán couldn't find his breath. His vision narrowed. Was this what a panic attack felt like?

"If she's okay, if she heals quickly, will they let her stay?"

For the first time since he'd met the man, Chance's smirk dissolved.

"I cannot answer that, Dr. Adler. But I encourage you to consider her role if they let her stay. Because one is adept at something does not mean they should be run ragged completing that task."

A deep unease slammed against Aiodhán's chest, settling there. Chance wasn't saying anything Aiodhán hadn't dragged himself over the coals thinking about the past couple hours.

It didn't matter how he made it right. Whatever she needed, he'd give her, even if it slowly killed him in the process.

Space from him.

Turning down the trauma center job.

"I know. I'll fix it. Whatever it takes, as long as she can stay. I… I asked her to help me run the trauma center across the street."

"Even though she came here to study women's health?"

"She can do that there, too. It's a trauma center with a wing dedicated to women who need access to care but no means."

"That sounds like a cause our princess would champion. But the choice is not only hers to make."

Chance gave his curt, telltale nod, and both men focused on the woman lying on the bed. None of it mattered if the princess—Emilia—wasn't well enough to continue following her dream to be a doctor. If her parents dragged her back to sell her like chattel to the wealthiest suitor.

His pager went off, breaking his spiraling thoughts.

"Her results are in."

"Go," Chance said. "I'll keep watch over her."

Aiodhán nodded and took off at a sprint to the lab. Somehow, whatever pull he'd felt toward Emilia before had doubled since she collapsed. She might have an entire country—hell, an army—to go to war for her, but damn if he didn't want to be counted among those.

What's that supposed to mean? You can't be with her.

No, he couldn't. And he shouldn't even care about her, because…because he could *lose* her. That was all he needed to distance himself.

The lab tech handed over a sealed manila envelope and Aiodhán closed his eyes. His hands shook as he tore open the envelope. He read the results and then read them again. Then a third time.

No. This can't be...

His stomach dropped to his feet, and his jaw clenched with worry. His teeth clattered even though the lab was warm.

"Has this been verified?" he asked the tech.

"We ran it through three times." The tech shrugged as if the results weren't life-changing. Damning.

Aiodhán did some quick calculations and shook his head. It'd been almost *four months* since he'd met Emilia at the bar. Sixteen weeks if the tally he kept in his head was right, not counting the passionate kiss they'd shared a month ago. If those results were accurate...

"Run them again. I'll wait."

"It could take up to fifteen minutes for the results."

"I'll wait," Aiodhán said again.

He paced the hall, growing more and more agitated. When the lab tech signaled him over, he snatched the paper from him. It was confirmed. *Oh, God*. He tucked the paper in his back pocket and strode back to her room.

Emilia was...

Which meant *he* was...

He was going to be a *dad*. He knew it was his, in the same way he'd sort of always known Emilia was special, different. Maybe he hadn't guessed she was a princess, but he'd known something. And he knew this.

Oh, *God*.

Forget the distance—he was all-in now, whether he wanted to be or not.

A barrage of questions hit him like punches from a prizefighter. Had she had medical care since she arrived? Would she be able to keep it? Would her husband back in Zephyranthes raise Aiodhán's kid? Would Aiodhán be expected to participate? Did he *want* to?

He didn't know. It was…it was everything he'd avoided his entire life. But on the other hand, it wasn't just a woman who'd snuck past his defenses. It was a *kid*. *His* kid. *Their* kid.

It wasn't about Aiodhán anymore.

Worry pressed against his chest, but he pushed it down where he could ignore it. One final question landed, a sucker punch as he reached Emilia's door.

Had she known about the pregnancy? Scientifically, it seemed impossible to not know about this for sixteen whole weeks. But if she *had* known…

No. She wouldn't have. That wasn't like her. But how much did he really know about the woman who'd captured his attention?

Very little, it seemed.

He might not have any of those answers, but one came to him with startling clarity.

Emilia needed to stay because if she went home to Zephyranthes, that was most likely the end of everything she cared about.

And quite possibly the same for him.

CHAPTER EIGHT

EMILIA'S EYES FLUTTERED OPEN. The view in front of her was immediately recognizable. The vantage point was not. She gazed up at the bright white lights she'd worked under for months now, the machines beeping and purring at her side like a familiar voice lulling her to sleep. But it was the soft bed beneath her, the warm blankets acting as a cocoon, the wires crisscrossing her body that were confusing.

"Why…" She swallowed, but it felt like her throat was laced with the sand outside her summer home on the Cantabrian Sea. "Why am I here?" The dryness didn't dissipate, and her eyes were sensitive to the intensity of the lights above.

"Emilia?" The voice was as familiar but as disorienting as the rest of the scene. She rolled her head to the side, and her lips parted in surprise. Aiodhán sat in a chair looking unkempt. His hair stood on end, and the stubble on his chin said he hadn't used a razor in at least a full day. It…suited him. She swallowed again, but now it felt like trying to coax knives down her throat.

She winced.

"Can I get you something? Water?"

She nodded, bringing light to other injuries. There was a sharp pain pulsing in her head, a dull ache emanating from it. What was Aiodhán doing here? What was *she* doing here?

"Ow," she whispered.

"Do you remember anything from yesterday?" She shook her head more gingerly, but it still throbbed.

"My head hurts. Did I hit it?"

Despite the discomfort it caused, she sat up and focused her gaze on Aiodhán as he nodded. His smile was thin and barely masked the hurt etched in his eyes. Had she messed something up with a patient? The only time he'd appeared as concerned was when she'd set up an OR in a way that wasn't his "usual layout." It was the only reason that made sense for him to be in her room.

"You passed out in the ER. Your head hit the ground pretty damn hard. You have a concussion, but it could have been worse." Was that a shudder that rolled through him?

Heat rose up her neck, spread to her cheeks. "Is my patient okay?"

"He's fine. You finished closing what most other interns wouldn't have been able to do in better condition, and you did a great job, Emilia."

Aiodhán's palm cupped her head, which was good, because she felt dizzy all of a sudden. She'd done well? And he'd actually admitted as much?

Before she could think about her health or why she might have collapsed in the middle of a hospital ER, the doors opened and the privacy curtain parted. Chance appeared, and though the man likely thought of her as a thorn in his side, hot tears built behind her eyes at the sight of someone from home. Someone who truly knew her.

"*Princesa*, you're looking better."

Well, she probably was, until the color drained from her face at the mention of her title. "Chance!"

Aiodhán intervened. "It's fine. I know." And there went the blood, racing back to her cheeks and neck, painting her the color of mortification.

"I'm sorry I didn't say anything. The chief medical officer agreed it was best if the staff not be made aware—"

"It's okay. I don't care about any of that, Emilia."

What alternate universe had she awoken in? Aiodhán knew who she was, that she'd been hiding that secret, and he didn't care? Something wasn't right…

"Now that you're aware of her status, sir, might I request that you refer to her as Your Royal Highness in private," Chance said.

"Absolutely not," Emilia said, sitting up straighter, mustering any semblance of courage and fortitude that might be hiding out in her body that ached everywhere. "You'll call me Emilia or de Reyes as you usually do, and Chance won't have anything to say about it."

"But—"

"I'm not *his* princess, Chance. Please, let me have my time here be as normal as it can be. That said, you probably have some questions about how we move forward with the staff. I'll be happy to give any insight I can."

The men looked at each other, and when Aiodhán dipped his chin to his chest, a chill tickled her skin.

"What? Have I been let go from the program because of my accident?"

"No, nothing like that. You're the top student, Emilia. I wouldn't kick you out unless…"

"Unless what?"

"I've contacted the king and queen, madam. They're concerned about your health here," Chance said.

"You shouldn't have done that, Chance. I'm fine, right, Aiodhán? Just tired."

The chills turned to icy tendrils of worry when Aiodhán began to pace the floor by her bedside.

"Can I have a moment alone with Emilia?" he asked.

"Need I remind you, Dr. Adler, that I have medical power of attorney—"

Emilia sighed. "If I'm unconscious or unresponsive. Neither of which I am. Please, Chance. Let me talk to him."

Chance bowed his head and left. The energy in the room was thick with tension.

"What is it, Aiodhán? You've always been straight with me, and I need that right now."

He slumped into the oversize chair she'd found him in when she awoke. Had she ever seen the man sit down? Once, when he laced up his shoes after their…night together. Beyond that, he was a workhorse, dragging the rest of them behind him. Anxiety jumped atop her nerve endings like they were springs.

When he didn't say anything, she spoke up. "Can you please tell me what the diagnosis is?"

"You're pregnant, Emilia."

"What? No," she whispered, her gaze somewhere beyond him. "No. I can't be. I'm—"

His lips opened as if he wanted to add something, but Chance poked his head in the room.

"They're here."

"Who is?"

"The king and queen," Chance said.

"My parents are where?" Emilia attempted to get out of bed, her head spinning with the sudden movement, the onslaught of information.

Her parents.

A baby.

Aiodhán's baby. She pressed the heels of her palms against her eyes. Aiodhán helped her lie back down.

"Please don't get up. You need your rest. And Chance, we need a minute."

"This is the king and queen. I don't plan on—"

"Chance. Please." He pointed to Emilia, whose lips trembled. She couldn't stop her teeth from chattering. "Trust me. We need a damned minute. Stall them," Aiodhán said.

She was grateful he spoke up for her. Somehow, she'd lost her voice. What could she possibly have to say in light of what she'd been told?

Aiodhán and Chance shared a look, but she couldn't comprehend it. Couldn't even try.

"I'll see what I can do." Chance left, and the room became silent again, save for the steady beep-beep of the machines in her room.

"Emilia, I am right that I am the father? You haven't been seeing anyone else?"

"Yes, of course," she whispered. "I'm not seeing anyone and haven't since you and I on that first night. Who has the time? I do my work, I come home and try for six hours of sleep, and go back to do it all again the next day. You know very well I don't have time for a social life. Not even those that happen in secret on-call rooms."

Aiodhán nodded, looking relieved and conflicted at the same time. Unease lingered around his eyes. "How are you? What can I do?"

She tried on a smile, her training superseding her biology.

"I don't know, honestly. I mean, I'm terrified, confused, and unsure how this even happened."

"Yeah, pretty much the same here. Especially that last part," he said, running a hand through his hair. "We used protection."

The corner of her lips quirked up.

"You're a brilliant doctor, Aiodhán. Go ahead and figure out the statistics on that while I wait."

He chuckled, lightening the mood enough she didn't feel as if she was suffocating. "What about your period? Didn't you realize something was off? It's been four months."

"It was light the first two months, and I didn't

have one at all this month. To be honest, I thought I was overworked and severely stressed."

"I'm so sorry, Emilia." He held out a hand, and she took it. Only then did a rogue tear fall on her cheek. He wiped it away. "We'll be okay, though. I don't know how, but I know we will be."

Her smile dissolved.

"There is no *we*, Aiodhán. There can't be. I told you that when you tried to kiss me again."

Aiodhán shook his head. "No. You said it wasn't fair. I'm your boss, Emilia, and I get it. I messed up so badly." He squeezed her hand, and her heart cracked.

"You're right. I said it wasn't fair, but not for the reason you think. I said it because I can't have a normal relationship. I'm a *princess*, Aiodhán. Which means I'm going to be the queen of Zephyranthes one day, married to the prince consort."

The look on Aiodhán's face made her wish she'd never met him in that bar. Because she'd fallen for him, too, that day. Not in love, but she'd felt a deep connection that only intensified working alongside him. Sure, he was a tough boss, but he was fair, too. And brilliant beyond measure. But in letting him in, even a little, she'd opened them up to this heartache.

"But the baby—"

"The baby doesn't change anything," she said. Her voice cracked.

"The baby changes *everything*." He kneeled at her side. "Emilia, *please*. Please hear me out. There's got to be a way we can fix this so we have a chance."

She straightened her shoulders. Aiodhán was an amazing man, if not overly dedicated to work. But how could she fault that, when she saw the impact he made on his patients day after day? He was thoughtful with his patients, brilliant as a surgeon, and passionate as a teacher. She'd been lucky to learn from him.

It warmed her heart that no matter what happened, she'd also carry a part of him with her forever, even if she couldn't have Aiodhán as anything more than a colleague.

And she couldn't have him, that much she knew with absolute certainty.

"A chance at what? You weren't ever interested in a relationship. Do you really think this could work, even if we weren't up against my crown and country?"

"Then, what do we do?"

"I get a checkup. I must be nearly midway through my pregnancy, and I've not had any medical care. Then…we face the king and queen. They'll want to—" her voice broke "—they'll want me to come home with them."

He shot up. "You can't. Not yet. You've got a year and a half left of your residency. And what am I supposed to do without you both?"

It was terribly inconvenient that the way Aiodhán's lips, twisted in pain, looked so good on him. Especially since they did so every time he was around her. In a different world, they might have had a chance together, if she weren't a princess with another life that awaited her. She was always going to be an interloper in this world of medicine. In Aiodhán's world.

But now there was a tether between the two. An uncuttable tether.

He was right on one count. The baby changed everything.

"Can I see the test results?" He handed her the paper in his pocket, which she read over. "I don't see a way to avoid leaving. But I'll never keep you from her."

"It's a girl?" he asked. She nodded, tears flowing freely down her cheeks now as she pointed that out on her test results.

"I'm far enough along they must be able to tell from the blood test."

"I must have missed that."

Aiodhán paced again, worrying his bottom lip between his teeth. She wanted to know what he was thinking, but that wasn't as important as giving him time to process this.

She'd felt the pressing weight of her obligations since she'd arrived in America on borrowed time. No matter what her parents dictated, she wouldn't be staying long either way. Still, she'd just gotten started—on her dream, on putting the nightmare of her mother's betrayal behind her…on building a life and that was distinctively *hers*.

And Aiodhán was a pawn in a game so much bigger than himself. She felt horrible for involving him.

"What do you want to do, Emilia?"

She looked up at him, her eyes prickling with tears and her bottom lip quivering.

"I don't know. I… I want to be a doctor. I want to lead my country, however that looks. This wasn't in my plans."

"Mine, either."

"We should talk about how to address my parents, Aiodhán."

He blanched. "You mean like *Your Majesty* and all that?"

She smiled. "That would be a great start, and it reminds me we need to talk about royal protocol in general, but no, that wasn't what I meant. How will we address the pregnancy?"

"I get a say in this?"

"Of course. You're the father. I wouldn't dream of taking your choice in the matter from you."

"Well, I want to keep it, too, if that's what you're asking. As for what it means for you and me, I have an idea."

"I'm open to anything at this point," she said.

He opened his mouth to reply when the door opened again and Bridget peeked through the curtain.

"Hey, there."

"Bridget," Emilia whispered. There went the tears again. Good grief, she was emotional of late, wasn't she? She'd be leaving so much more than a job and the man she cared about when she went home. "It's so good to see you."

"Yeah. Ditto. Except you look like hell."

"*Bridget*," Aiodhán chided her.

"What? She does." Bridget sat on the edge of the bed, missing Aiodhán's withering look. "Anyway, I just wanted to check on you. There's some powerful-looking people right behind me. Are you involved with the feds?"

Emilia laughed. It felt good, after all the serious talk. That certainly wasn't over, but she needed joy while she could get it.

"You can let them in," she said.

The door opened, and sure enough, her father and stepmother strode through the door. Chance followed close behind. They were tall, elegant, *polished*. They stuck out like lilies in a field of dandelions. One wasn't better, just…more regal.

What did that make her? Only one answer made sense in that moment, as she hugged her father tight.

"Bridget, Aiodhán, please let me introduce you to the king and queen of Zephyranthes, my parents."

CHAPTER NINE

"EMILIA…" WHISPERED HER FATHER, the king. He ignored the other two in the room, but Aiodhán knew he'd do the same if his daughter was in trouble. His daughter… He swallowed hard, risking a glance at Emilia's abdomen where his future grew. "Are you all right?"

The king wore a bespoke gray designer suit and was an inch shorter than Aiodhán, but sturdier. He looked like he might have lifted with Arnold Schwarzenegger back in the day. But it was his eyes that had Aiodhán staring. They were the same green as Emilia's, a jade-meets-the-Atlantic-after-a-storm color but with age lines fanning out from them. The woman was younger and didn't resemble Emilia at all. It was only then Aiodhán recalled that she was Emilia's stepmother.

A small gap opened in Aiodhán's chest. The concern her dad felt for her would most certainly evaporate the minute she let them in on why she was in a hospital bed instead of caring for a patient in one.

"I'm fine, Father. But we should talk."

Bridget slipped out the door without making a noise.

Aiodhán dipped his head low in greeting, as he'd seen Chance do. It might not be exactly right, but surely he couldn't be blamed for not knowing how to greet actual royalty. Royalty who would be his child's grandparents.

Wait…did that make the baby a princess?

Oh, God, he'd screwed this up royally. *Royally. Ha!*

"Your Majesty… Majesties. I'm Aiodhán Adler. Welcome to the United States, to Minneapolis. To our hospital."

Saying that out loud reminded him who he was. It'd been easy to forget his own power, worth, and choice in learning that Emilia was a member of the royal family. But he wasn't a slouch. And she was carrying his daughter. He stood up straighter.

"Aiodhán is in charge of the residents," she said, when her parents simply nodded at his introduction. Her voice was strong and regal. How hadn't he realized she was a princess before? Or at least a duchess or something similar. Her posture, the way she spoke and listened…

The man started rattling off concerns in Zephyr, the thick, syrupy language beautiful but incomprehensible to Aiodhán, even with his limited high school Spanish.

"*Papá*," Emilia said. She glanced around the room, jutting her chin out toward the others.

"Of course. Apologies," her father continued in English. "Let's get you home first, then our own doctors can find out what's going on with you." He looked back at Aiodhán. "No offense, Doctor, but we've got physicians on staff who can take better care of her."

For the second time that day, he was speechless. His mind and heart struggled to reconcile their conflicting feelings about Emilia's test results. But that was nothing compared to the other implications. He'd unknowingly created a new line of succession in a country he knew nothing about, except it was somewhere in the Mediterranean.

On one hand, this new information was life-ending, or life-altering at least, which for him might as well be the same thing. He didn't want to burden Emilia with his all-encompassing need to work away any residual longing for a family of his own that lived rent-free in his chest.

On the other hand, this was *Emilia* he was talking about. And they'd made a *child*. It was kind of amazing, in a terrifying, stomach-dropping kind of way.

But it wasn't as if he'd knocked up a physician from Minneapolis. He'd gotten the princess of a European country pregnant out of wedlock. She'd said she wanted to know his ideas, his choice. That really was just an illusion though, wasn't it? A baby—a live, growing child was at stake here.

Yet…all of that wasn't as big a concern as what her father had said. He did, indeed, want to take Emilia home. Yeah, that wasn't happening. He might not be willing to love and care for someone in a traditional way—a lifetime of fighting against that had left his heart atrophied in that way. But he could help her stay, and maybe, just maybe, give him a way to see his daughter grow up.

Emilia couldn't have a real relationship, and he

couldn't, either. They were, in that way, perfect for one another.

"I'm not so sure about that," Aiodhán said, his voice thick. A silence fell over the room, but Aiodhán didn't care if that was the first time anyone had dared disagree with the king. This was Aiodhán's hospital, and Emilia was carrying *his* baby. "Your Majesty, I'm the chief of general surgery and the trauma center director. We run a damn fine program here, and Emilia is an incredible asset. I'd like to talk to you both about the ways we can care for her so she can continue her career."

"Her career?" The king frowned. "Her career is serving her country and fulfilling her duty as the crown princess of Zephyranthes. This was a professional-growth opportunity. But seeing as how it's making her sick—"

"Father, that's not it," Emilia said. The king's face turned as red as the alarm bells outside the room. "Rebecca, it's good to see you," Emilia added.

The woman dipped her head in Emilia's direction but refrained from any other emotional reaction. Her father, on the other hand, issued a directive to Emilia, again in Zephyr.

"Doctor, I'll sign whatever forms you need, even if it's against medical advice. We're taking our daughter home, and that's the end of it."

Aiodhán bristled. They hadn't asked her what she wanted, how her studies were going...*nothing*.

"Do you trust me?" he whispered to Emilia. She nodded up at him. He'd not had a chance to run this idea by her, but they didn't have time for that. It threw a wrench in his own plans, but that ship had sailed the day he met Emilia in the bar anyway. He took a deep breath and wrapped Emilia's hand back in his.

"I think we need to consider what Emilia wants in all of this," Aiodhán said. "This is her life, and I'll bet if you asked her, she'd call this life more than just a hobby. She wants to be a physician, and in my opinion we should get out of her way and let that happen. The world will be a better place with her caring hands available for patients."

The king's jaw clenched along with his fists. Aiodhán saw how he'd be a force to reckon with if someone came after what was his. But Emilia wasn't anyone's.

Chance stood back, a barely visible smile pulling at his lips. That meant Aiodhán was on the right track. He took her hand in his.

"Just who do you think you are?"

Aiodhán straightened his shoulders and glanced down at Emilia. She nodded and squeezed his hand, encouraging him. "I'm the father of the baby Emilia is carrying, and if she'll have me—" he said, kneeling on one knee. He wished it was more difficult to imagine he was doing this for real. "I'd like to marry her and be her proud husband."

CHAPTER TEN

THE ROOM ERUPTED into pandemonium. Her father's face just erupted, period. She schooled her features so the shock didn't register on her face. She'd expected Aiodhán to share the pregnancy, but what he'd actually done—*proposed?*

"Tell me he's kidding, *hija*," her father said. "After Luis—"

"He's *nothing* like Luis, Papa. Now, if you'll listen to us—"

"Why should I, Emi? You come here to pursue medicine, or so you say. But then I get a call that you're injured at work, only to arrive and find you're *embarazada...*"

"She doesn't have anything to be embarrassed about," Aiodhán said. Emilia bit back a grin because none of this was funny. But it was erring toward so tragic it became comedic.

"He means *pregnant*, Aiodhán," she said through gritted teeth.

"Oh." Her betrothed—or whatever she should call him since he hadn't really asked her anything, and she certainly hadn't said yes to his ridiculous proposal—said.

Start him on Zephyr lessons immediately.

Emilia adjusted in her bed. She was still on bed rest until more tests came back on the health of the baby she hadn't known she carried until moments earlier.

Her parents murmured to one another in clipped Zephyr she was too far away to hear. She had to admit she preferred their yelling to the hushed whispers.

"Fine," her father said. "Tell me your plan, then. Because it's obvious this wasn't a planned pregnancy."

Aiodhán stiffened beside her. "No," she said. Not to her father, who would believe her no matter what, but to Aiodhán. If he thought her capable of that kind of duplicity... "No, it wasn't planned."

Aiodhán squeezed her hand. His strength buoyed her.

"Your Majesties, I know it's quite a shock to be greeted with this kind of news the minute you've arrived, but we're committed to making it work and could use your support to do so."

"To making what work? A marriage? Do either of you have any idea what kind of commitment a good, strong marriage between *equals* takes? What raising a child in this world might require?"

Emilia cringed at the word *equals*. In so many ways Aiodhán was hers, if only her title and royal lineage could be taken out of the equation.

They both dreamt of a life of service to others in the medical field, they both were dedicated, hard workers, and as he'd mentioned, they were committed to making sure they gave their all to their unexpected gift.

A gift it was, too. Emilia was surer of that than anything else in her life.

"I do," Aiodhán said. She shot him a glance. What was he doing? She'd assumed the proposal was fake, a way to buy them time, but there went Aiodhán, telling her parents they had a plan in place. She hadn't even said yes. "To be honest, I never believed in love. To me, that word only equaled loss. But my friend convinced me to come to his wedding. If I hadn't, I wouldn't have met Emilia at the bar that night, and I wouldn't know the amazing passion your daughter holds for medicine, for life, and for her family. I know I have a lot to learn, but I'm willing to learn it. For her. For our daughter."

Emilia took in a sharp breath. She only released it when her father's frown softened ever so slightly along the edges. He sighed, and she, in turn, released the breath she'd been holding.

"You love her, then?"

"To be honest, sir, try as I did to avoid it, I care about her more than I've cared about anything in a long time. I want a life with Emilia and the child we've created, whatever that looks like." When he gazed over at her, she saw the truth in his statement and it simultaneously warmed her while sending shivers racing across her skin. What would happen if they went through with this—real or not—and she went back to Zephyranthes? Would he follow? What would he do there? The pressure was too much to put on him. But for now, it was nice to hear romantic words she never imagined she'd hear. "Like I said, we didn't plan on any of this, but I'll never let anything happen to either of them. I'll do what it takes."

Emilia's father and stepmother shared a glance, and Rebecca gave a dignified, subtle nod. It was hopeful.

"I see. I can see your dedication to my daughter, especially given the condition she's in because of you."

Emilia opened her mouth to object—like Aiodhán said, it took two of them to get here—but he'd already jumped in.

"And I'll make that right. Whatever it takes."

He squeezed her hand again, and heat built behind her eyes. If only this were real. She'd never wanted a family or love before, only because she'd assumed that wasn't in her cards: if she married, it would be for duty. But now...now she dared to wish for more than a life where she could love her duty to her country. She wanted love, period.

"Papa, can Aiodhán and I have a moment together? We've barely said hello to one another since my accident, and I need... I need to take a breath."

Rebecca and the king stood.

"We'll be right outside," her dad said.

Emilia nodded. "Thank you. I know you traveled a long way to see me and that you've been worried. So we'll be quick."

"Fine, fine."

When they were alone, Emilia glanced up at Aiodhán, who still held her hand.

"You can let go, you know. They're gone."

"What if I don't want to?"

She sighed and took her hand back. "Aiodhán, why would your idea include something as permanent as marriage? What the heck were you thinking?"

He leaned down, his breath hot on her neck. "To save you from going back there."

"*There* is my home, Aiodhán, and those are my parents—"

"Who want to sell you off to the highest bidder. While you're pregnant with my baby. They didn't even flinch when I asked if they'd still consider ripping you from this life you love."

He wasn't telling her anything that wasn't true. And maybe five months ago, fresh out of the media scrutiny around her mother and betrayal of Luis, she'd have agreed. But she loved her home. Looked forward to her duty. Sure, she had reservations about marrying someone she'd never met, but it's not like she could upend centuries of tradition just because she'd fallen for a commoner.

She gazed up at him, noticing the small tick in his jaw. She also took a minute to appreciate his strength and the gentle way he used his thumbs to rub circles on the heel of her palm. What she tried to ignore? The uniquely Aiodhán scent of soap and pine that worked its way past her defenses and made her woozy in a different way.

The kind of way that made her *want* to upend tradition.

"I'm sorry about that. I really am. But all I wanted

was to guarantee you have time to make a decision you're comfortable with. You wanted something that would keep you here. Well, being my fiancée was all I could come up with in the thirty seconds we had to hatch a plan. It wasn't the perfect solution, but it's a start. You can still say no, you know. To being my fiancée."

Her pulse slowed enough she could catch her breath. She had asked for that, and to his credit he'd put himself in a terrible position just to help her. He just as easily could have run from this since it wasn't his concern, not really. But then, the idea of what would happen after his announcement made her shudder. "Perhaps you're right. But what is your plan, exactly? To marry me and make an honest woman out of me? I mean, you can barely stand to be around me most days."

He gazed down at her.

"That's not true, Emilia. Not even close. I just…" Nerves floated to the surface of her skin, making it itch. "I didn't know who you were when we spent that night together. When you showed up at the hospital that day, I didn't know if I could work alongside you and keep my feelings at bay. I think you saw how bad I was at it that day I…"

"The day you kissed me good and long enough I forgot my own name?"

He smiled, and her heart rate sped up. That was decidedly against doctor's orders, so she tried to get her mind off that searing kiss. What was her future without him?

Flying back home, a secret tucked away from her country.

Walking down the aisle toward a man she neither knew nor was capable of loving.

Saying goodbye to Aiodhán forever. Raising her baby alone. *Their baby*, she reminded herself again.

"Yep. That day. I tried to ignore the other feelings as they'd crop back up, but watching you work and laugh and be an amazing doctor isn't exactly a recipe for turning off how I feel for you."

"You feel things for me? Other than the obvious physical stuff?" She'd—wrongly?—assumed their fiery passion was a one-night thing, at least on his part. When he kissed her, she'd concluded he still wanted more of that. But to hear how he watched her work, appreciated more than her body, and without knowing her title…it was dizzying. Also against doctor's orders. "That's why you talked to me about moving past our night together that first day of work."

His smile warmed the parts of her that felt cold and exposed since the results of her tests had come back.

"Yeah. I sorta had to make that call. Survival, you know?" She did. It's why she'd offered to take extra shifts and longer hours: if she were wholly exhausted, she wouldn't have to let her mind wander to the handsome doctor in charge of her future as an OB resident. And what that doctor happened to look and feel and taste like bared for her greedy hands and lips. "But I guess it's for the best I did, now that I know who you are. Neither of us can have a traditional relationship, but maybe this is the best of both worlds."

She paused, giving herself a three count until she faked a laugh. Their love of medicine was the only thing they had in common.

"How is that? Because I don't see any way this actually works, Aiodhán. I mean, maybe we keep the pretense of an engagement up, but then when my parents leave we can—"

"No. I don't want to cut it off. I want to marry you, Emilia. Maybe we're not traditional, but I care for you—despite my best efforts not to," he said, winking. She laughed, but her chest rose and fell with nervousness. The beeping behind her picked up pace, likely from her pulse skyrocketing.

"Okay, so tell me what you mean."

"I mean we're perfect together because you can't have a so-called real relationship. You're sworn to your country and crown. And I can't give you traditional romance. I think I've worked too hard to surgically remove that part from my heart since I lost my parents. So if we go into this with realistic expectations, I think we can make it work."

Emilia couldn't believe it, but she was nodding. On paper, at least, that made perfect sense.

"We don't have to tell your parents all of that, just that we are committed to making this work for our daughter and our careers."

Emilia's cheeks flashed with heat. "What about—"

"Sex?" he asked. She nodded, biting her bottom

lip. He surprised her with a kiss. "I don't know. Is that something you're interested in?"

"I'm not *not* interested," she said, smiling. The heat on her cheeks—and south—told a similar story.

"Fair enough." He laughed. "Any more questions in that beautiful brain of yours?" he asked. The heat intensified. She could get used to this attention, even as she knew she shouldn't.

"Just one." He kissed her again, almost making her forget. "Where will you live?"

"With you, if you'll have me. I'm guessing your apartment isn't a sparsely furnished studio like mine."

She shook her head. "Nope. One of the perks of being royalty. I have a rather nice apartment, actually, and would love to have you." Oh, my goodness. Reality set in as she realized she'd just said she wanted to move in with Dr. Aiodhán Adler. "But that's actually not what I meant. Will you follow us back to Zephyranthes?"

Aiodhán glanced at his lap. "I… I don't know, to be honest. I hadn't thought that far. I mean, I don't know anything about your country—"

"I'll teach you, of course. I'd never let you go if you weren't aware of our culture or language or customs."

"The language. I also hadn't thought about that. Man, I really jumped the gun, didn't I?"

Emilia felt his fear, could understand it on a cellular level. He'd thrown his whole future on the proverbial sword. For her. So she could stay and pursue her dream. He might not be royal by blood, but he was her white knight.

"You can still change your mind." But she didn't want him to. A small part of her—small enough she'd never admit it outside her own head—wanted to see where this went. Maybe there was a chance she would get the happily ever after she'd thought was forbidden.

Aiodhán leaned in. "I don't want to. It's just a lot to think about. If you don't mind helping talk me through some of the logistics, I'm in, Emilia. I mean that."

"Thank you, Aiodhán. For giving up so much to take care of me."

"I should have done it sooner. But I'm here now. Should we bring the king and queen back in?" She nodded. "I never thought I'd say those words out loud, by the way."

Emilia laughed again. She might be in a hospital bed, carrying a surprise pregnancy, but she was… happy. For the first time in a long time, maybe since she was seven, she had a sense of what life could offer her, and it was beautiful.

"Before they come in, you should know my parents will pull out all the stops. We won't be able to hide from the crown's influence or presence in our lives."

"I figured as much. It will be the same here. We'll have to start with HR here at Minnie Gen and let them know we're engaged. We might have been able to avoid that before, since we'd slept together before you were my intern, but it's protocol to disclose all consensual relationships between staff. You might get reassigned to another physician for your residency. That might take the trauma job off the table, but you'll still be able to practice."

"That's fine. That's all I need." *For now.* Aiodhán made her want things she'd never considered before… Her heart's desire took a different shape in a brief daydream in which Aiodhán wrapped his arms around her from behind, resting his palms on her swollen stomach. They were in their own home, flamenco music playing softly on speakers behind them, and he swayed his body against hers, kissing her neck while they danced barefoot.

"I'll make sure you get more than what you need. I want to take care of you and our child, Emilia."

Heat crept up her neck at being caught wishing for things that were wholly impossible.

Our child.

A wave of dizziness washed over Emilia. As much as it pained her to admit it, she needed him to get through whatever her life looked like next. So long as she could keep the pesky daydreams at bay, it wouldn't be too difficult to do that.

"Thank you," she whispered.

"Of course," he replied, helping her lie back in bed before finding a seat beside her. "How are you feeling?"

She tilted her head to each side. "All right, I guess. A little tired, and my head is sore, but otherwise normal."

"We need to get you seen by the team, Emilia. I know you'll want to keep this under wraps, but—"

"No. I agree. The baby's safety matters more than anything else. And this team, the Gold Fleece Foundation doctors—they're why I'm here."

"Okay, we'll set it up for tomorrow."

"Emilia, I'd like to talk now, if you two are done," her father said, poking his head in.

Emilia sighed but didn't take her hand off her belly. It offered her strength, reminded her why she was there and why standing their ground was important. It wasn't just her life at stake now; she owed freedom to her daughter.

"Yes, of course," she said, even if she wanted to close her eyes and sleep for a week.

When everyone was settled, her father dove in.

"We can't take him back to Zephyranthes," the king said. "Not like this. Not while the media is still hungry for information about your mother. They're looking for anything that would paint our family in a negative light. You know that, Emi."

She did. It was always that way: the monarchy wasn't a popular idea with some of the country. With poverty and homelessness on the rise due to global inflation, she understood. Even Aiodhán had his doubts about the necessity of royalty in the modern age. But she knew what others didn't: international relations relied on their political expertise, and their charity patronage donated to causes that kept citizens clothed and housed. Even the top-tier education in Zephyranthes was funded by the monarchy, and each of the hospitals required no supplemental insurance thanks to her family's donations.

They did good work, but unless they took credit for all of that—something her father refused to do—they were bound to receive criticism.

"What do you suggest?" Rebecca asked. It was the first time she'd spoken. Emilia wanted to know what her stepmother must be thinking. She'd tried and tried in vain to get pregnant, only to be left without a child of her own, an heir for the throne.

And Emilia had had sex once—*once!*—in her life and gotten knocked up even with birth control. The unfairness of all of this knew no bounds.

"We create a story for the media they can't find fault in. A sympathetic story the country will believe. Princess studies in America, only to fall in love with a working-class man. It certainly isn't the first time such a thing has happened."

"And then what?" she asked. She *needed* to stay. Not just for herself anymore but to give Aiodhán time to figure out his place in her royal life.

"We give you two time here, working together, appearing for press engagements, items like that. Say a month. Prove this is more than a flash in the pan."

Okay. A month was something, at least.

"Then you two will marry in a public ceremony," he said. Emilia's blood ran cold. This was really happening. "She will continue her work here until the baby is born. We then bring you both back to begin your rule from there, the heir a part of its family."

He waved his hand as if the rest of it was inconsequential. As if her and Aiodhán's futures were inconsequential.

Aiodhán's hand tightened on her shoulder and she couldn't contain her nerves. She'd wanted to go back, to live in Zephyranthes and raise a family there. But after her residency. When she'd had time to live.

"We'll offer our support in the name of love, of course, and tomorrow we'll announce the pregnancy and how pleased we are to welcome the next in line for the throne."

"The throne," Aiodhán whispered. Emilia wished she could see his face above hers. Wished she could cup his cheeks and tell him it would all be a lot, yes, but it would be okay in the end. She wouldn't let him go through this alone.

But how could she say this when her parents left her in the hospital room for the evening, chatting about details and governor's visits and so many other items that made Emilia feel as if this were snowballing out of her control?

How could she convince her husband-to-be that it would be okay if she didn't believe it herself?

CHAPTER ELEVEN

AIODHÁN GLANCED DOWN at his tie. It felt more like a noose.

"Isn't there a loophole in a royal decree that might get us off the hook for this?" he asked.

Emilia smiled up at him and a little of the panic that had raced through his veins slowed, dissolving into his bloodstream and allowing him a moment's peace.

"Unfortunately not. This is just part of the rigmarole. I wish I could say it's the hardest part of this transition, but that's not even remotely true."

"Um…thanks, Em. Love the vote of confidence." He faked a laugh, but it sounded as hollow as he felt. It wasn't like he hadn't known what he'd been getting himself into. He'd seen enough movies, read enough books to know that monarchies were a different breed. Meetings, classes, language lessons— all of it had been expected. But rubbing elbows with Emilia's family all week had made him into a phony—an unexplored side effect he hadn't considered when it came to caring about someone else.

Sure, it was impossible to constantly worry he could lose them—and he did. Every damned accident victim brought through the ER bay threw him into a spiral. Was it Emilia? He didn't know how he was supposed to let that go, even when he kept telling himself it was okay, she knew he had trouble with letting people in.

But worse than all of that was a new kind of fear as he slid into being Emilia's partner…

Being seen for who he really was.

He might be a stellar surgeon, physician, and scientist, but what else did he have to offer? Especially when he'd already witnessed his bride-to-be undergo a rapid transformation from overworked resident to a glowing, pregnant princess?

"Look this way," Paulo, part of the royal entourage, said, tugging at Aiodhán's sleeve. He did as he was told.

This was going to be a disaster, wasn't it?

When Emilia reached up on her toes and kissed him, though, he exhaled.

"It's you and me," she whispered, triggering their shared mantra.

"And our little bean." Okay, this was fine. Just another meeting, and he'd be doing it with her by his side. Regardless of how they'd arrived where they were—engaged and headed to the altar, then the throne, with an unplanned pregnancy—they were there together. And together was the only way to the other side of this, he was damned sure of that much. If his life looked different, that was fine as long as he could go to bed knowing he'd done the right thing.

Right now that meant cutting his hair, trimming his beard, and getting fitted for a suit. He didn't *do* suits, not when more than half his life was in scrubs.

All for a single press conference and dinner with the governor of Minnesota.

He straightened his tie when Paulo's back was turned. Not one damned day in his life had he given his appearance any thought, aside from whether he looked professional or not. But now he had two stylists fussing over him, and he didn't like it.

"You look great," she said. "And I promise you will get used to this. It'll become part of the background to our lives."

He wasn't sure that made things any better.

"Okay, quiz me again," he said, ignoring the pervasive intrusion of the other stylist—what his name? George? Tomas?

"The royal values?"

"Family, country, loyalty."

"In Zephyr?" He glanced at her as Paulo put his tie back to where he wanted it. Aiodhán wished like hell he'd paid more attention to Spanish studies in school. Maybe then he could at least fake Zephyr enough not to be a total fraud. He could tell her each muscle in the human body, what they did, how they performed together, but he couldn't recall the first three words she'd taught him in her native tongue? He was failing her already. She waved him off. "Okay, we'll save that for later. But crest?"

"A crown on a field of blue, the green sea with fish and other sea creatures—"

"Symbolizing?"

He smiled. This he could answer, thanks to a very convincing study session where he got to kiss her wherever on her body she pointed if he got the question right. Maybe he'd draw her into another lesson that evening.

They were the only parts of his days that brought him any peace, curling up with Emilia. That had to count for something.

"The abundance Zephyranthes has to offer its citizens and its largest export, seafood." Truth be told, the more he learned about Emilia's country, the less he was worried about moving there. It seemed like an amazing place, and in the middle of a Midwest winter, time on the Mediterranean didn't seem like the worst idea.

As long as he forgot the other aspect of moving there: he'd be Emilia's husband. The prince consort of Zephyranthes.

"Hmmm. How about the line of succession?"

"Too easy. The king and queen, of course. You, next. Our daughter after that, and somewhere down the line, the dukes and duchesses on your father's side. I'll be a throw pillow on the throne—I'll look like one of the other pillows, but serve no actual use."

Sort of. The king and queen had been careful not to cross those lines, but he'd come pretty damned close the night before to being forced to choose between his job and his future family.

Emilia laughed. The sound was like soft rain on a warm afternoon. "Good job, future husband."

"Thanks, future wife." He leaned down to kiss her, and like always happened when they were close, he felt his pulse speed up and his body calm. She was like a lethal shot of adrenaline mixed with serotonin. He couldn't shake his new addiction to the drug that was Emilia de Reyes.

Aiodhán tucked a curl behind her ear. The scarlet waves were soft, but the color gave them an edge that made his breathing come a little faster. Kinda like the rest of the alluring woman—forgiving but with a determination that advertised her strength.

"I don't know how I didn't see right through those scrubs when I first met you." He paused and glanced around the palatial room with vaulted ceilings and crown molding that had to be turn-of-the-century. The lavish apartment was befitting a woman as dignified as Emilia. Funny how it took a woman from another country to show him places in his own city he hadn't known existed.

"I'm pretty sure you did." She winked.

"Not like that." He laughed, although there was a ring of truth to how he'd imagined her curves beneath those scrubs. "I mean, how didn't I recognize how regal you are? How you lead everyone with a simple smile. Your country is lucky. Hell, I'm lucky."

Another truth, one that dug into his self-imposed No Real Feelings wall and cracked it.

The way Emilia bit the corner of her lip made Aiodhán's heart beat hard against his ribs. It took all his restraint not to take her lip between his own teeth. Kissing Emilia with the hunger he felt wouldn't get them started on the right foot before the conference. He settled for a simple peck on the lips.

Paulo chastised them. "No kissing with her makeup finished. Save it for later." Aiodhán rolled his eyes. He might have to cut his hair and upgrade his wardrobe, but he'd damn well kiss his fiancée whenever he saw fit. It was the only perk in this whole arrangement.

"This is weird, huh? How quickly things changed between us?" he asked.

"It is. I'm glad to know you haven't hated me this whole time. I wouldn't be able to bear this, even temporarily, if I thought you despised me."

"Not even close, Emilia. I'll admit, you drive me to the edge of madness, but it isn't all bad."

"Ha ha, mister. You're funny when you're stressed, you know that?" She stepped off the pedestal and walked toward the exit. He considered that. He did rely on crappy, ill-timed humor when he was worried. She saw through him, just as he'd worried. He only prayed she liked what she saw. "And I love that about you. I love so many things about you."

The smile that spread over Aiodhán's face was the first genuine one he'd had in a while.

"And I think I have a plan for getting you to learn Zephyr. I'll give you an anatomy lesson later..." She winked at him. "With me as the mannequin since that seems to motivate you."

Heat flashed across his skin. What a whirlwind, to deeply desire this life with her one minute, then revolt against parts of it—namely the royalty portions—the next.

"You're onto something there."

"Like I mentioned earlier, I'm quite smart."

He squeezed her hand.

"You are. I wasn't ever in doubt there."

"So I've given you more information about my country and family over the past week than anyone should have to hear. Tell me about you. So far, all I know is that you're a tough boss, a brilliant surgeon, and—" she smiled "—that you've taken on a life of solitude so you can focus on medicine and not break any hearts in the process. Am I close?"

His laugh was stale. Again, he was struck by how deeply she saw through him. More like he didn't want his own heart to break any more than it already had. "More or less. But it's more—"

"Complicated?" He smiled and gave a curt nod. "I figured as much. What happened?"

The smile fell.

"My father died when I was eleven."

"Oh, my. I'm so sorry. How did he pass?"

"He got into a car wreck when he was too tired to drive one night. Ran off the road into a lake."

"Oh, Aiodhán, I'm so sorry."

"No, I mean thanks, but I'm not the only kid who had to go through that. Working at the ER every day, I'm reminded how normal my story actually is. Either way, it left a permanent scar that I never got over. I knew then and there I wanted to practice medicine so I could prevent other families from that kind of loss. Though, I think we both know it doesn't work like that."

"No, it doesn't. What about your mother?" Emilia had grown serious.

The stylists left them alone in the room, a gift, since Aiodhán's eyes burned with grief, even after all these years. That was the thing about loss. It stayed with you, tinted everything that followed a shade darker.

"She died, too. Years later, but also in a wreck. I'm not sure if you recall me talking about the I-35 bridge collapse?"

Emilia nodded and rubbed his hand affectionately. "The one you mentioned that day in the ER when the ten victims were brought in? That was my first day of residency."

"That's the one. My mother was one of the hundred-plus victims with severe injuries, and she died a few days later from them. It was my first month as a resident."

"That's awful."

He shrugged. "Now you know why I haven't let anyone in. Till you and the bean, anyway. The idea of losing you two is suffocating."

Emilia wrapped him in a bear hug and squeezed him tight.

"I understand that, you know."

He cleared his throat, which had gotten thick with decades of old emotions brought up from the depths. "Your family?"

Emilia chewed on her lip. "My mother."

"That's why you chose obstetrics?" A subtle nod had his chest constricting. Is this what it would feel like every time someone he cared about hurt? Like his chest was jolted by AED paddles? He didn't think he could take it.

"She died giving birth to my brother, and I never even got to meet him."

"God, I can't even imagine losing both in one day."

She waved him off. "It's okay. Well, actually it *was*." Emilia sat on the oversize love seat. "The man my father mentioned? Luis? He was my fiancé until he found out the child my mom was carrying wasn't the king's. He sold the information to the press, so I had to find out along with six million other Zephyranthians that my mother wasn't the woman—or queen—we all thought she was."

"Holy—" Aiodhán had to hand it to the monarchy. They took normal human problems and ratcheted them up a couple notches. "That's why your father is so worried about me and this, um, fast engagement."

"Yeah. More than what he said the other day about the media, he's worried about me. I can see it in his eyes, that he isn't sure I can take another heartache like that."

"I know you're strong enough to withstand any storm, Emilia, but I hope you know I'll block as many as I can for you. I may not have much to offer, but I can do that, at least."

"Thank you, Aiodhán. I believe you mean that. I just know the waves coming our way might make you rethink this whole arrangement. Being a part of this world, this life—I was *born* into it and have had time to fall in love with the opportunities it affords me. Choosing to be a part of it means giving up so much of what you used to be, and I don't want to ask that of you. I *can't* ask it."

Aiodhán gestured to his gelled, coiffed hair, his tailored suit, and his clean-shaven face.

"You didn't have to ask me, Emilia. I'm doing this because we made a child together, and she deserves parents who will do anything to keep her safe."

He couldn't read her smile but noted it didn't meet her eyes.

"We still really don't know much about each other, do we?" she asked.

He laughed, despite himself. "No, we don't. On one hand, you're surprising me around every turn, but on the other…" His gaze fell to her full lips, and he traced them with the pad of his thumb. She gave a barely audible gasp. "I know so much about you."

"Like what?" she whispered.

Aiodhán sat on the edge of the king-size bed then sank into the down-filled pillow beside her. The edge of his palm slid down her cheek in a caress that made him half-hard, a side effect that wasn't helped by the crimson glow on Emilia's cheeks, either. He'd done so well to keep this line drawn between them. But they'd agreed to take it as the moments arose and decide then. So he'd just let her decide what she wanted.

Please let it be me.

Like he'd said, he didn't have much to offer, but

this—keeping the smile on Princess Emilia de Reyes's lips?—he'd do anything for.

"Like how your skin announces everything you feel with a different color red. This," he said, touching the nape of her neck that was a cherry color, "is when you're embarrassed."

"You're sure about that?" she asked.

"Mmm-hmm. I'd bet my salary I'm right. And the light pink from a minute ago? You were happy."

"I was." Her breath hitched when Aiodhán's fingertips traced the green lace of her nightgown. "What am I now?" she asked. Her gaze melted into his and anything halfway about his erection went out the two-story window with the pale flush of dark pink covering the top of her breasts, just visible above the lace.

"Aroused. You want me to keep going, I think."

"My body seems to agree."

"And your head?" he asked, cupping her breast through the thin satin. He teased the bud of her swollen nipple between his thumb and finger, and she moaned with pleasure.

"It's kind of quiet in there right now."

"How about your heart?" he asked, spreading his palm and fingers across her chest.

"It's racing. I think you might be right about what it wants."

Aiodhán leaned over Emilia, sliding her beneath him. He dipped his head so that his lips brushed hers softly.

"Are you sure about this? I don't want to confuse things, but goddamn do I want you, Emilia."

She nodded, the blush on her bared skin dappled with moisture. He kissed her again, this time tracing her lips with his tongue, tasting the vanilla from her coffee. Even since finding out she was pregnant, she wasn't ever without a cup of it, even if she had switched to decaf. She claimed it was her Zephyr heritage.

"I want you, too," she said, breathless. "There's no reason we can't enjoy one another while we figure out our new life. If it doesn't work out, we can do what all the other royals do."

He kissed her neck. "Trash one another publicly and have torrid affairs?"

She giggled and shook her head, even as his lips traced her earlobe. The gasp she released almost made him come right there.

"No, keep separate bedrooms and pretend everything is fine."

He laughed, his forehead touching hers, his hands wandering over her frame while she arched her back, pressing her chest against his. She pulled his bottom lip between her teeth and sucked on it.

"Tonight, Emilia, there's no way we're sleeping in separate beds."

He teased her lips open with his tongue and finally sated the desire that had been building for months, since the last time he'd tasted this delicious woman in the on-call room.

If only he could silence his own head and heart

that were whining loudly that they still weren't ready to let anyone in. But it was too late; there was no going back to the man he'd been before Emilia. She'd dug her way through all of his walls and set up a home in his heart.

If he lost her, or the baby, there was no telling the husk of a man he'd become. All he could do was work like hell to make sure that never happened.

CHAPTER TWELVE

"OH, AIODHÁN!" EMILIA let out a gasp of pleasure so divine, she wasn't sure it was legal, even in the United States. "Please. Please keep going."

His fingers slid along her lace undergarments, and one slipped beneath the fabric, flicking her sensitive center. She moaned and lifted her hips in response.

"You mean this?" he asked, dipping two fingers into her warm, wet folds.

"Mm.... Yes!"

"I aim to please, Your Highness." He traced the curve of her breast with his tongue, finally sucking the swollen tip into his mouth. Emilia hadn't ever known such exquisite pleasure was possible. Aiodhán's hands and tongue were medicinal, curing all that ailed her. Her worries, insecurities, and the predicament surrounding her pregnancy all dissolved with his expert touch and kisses.

"I want you," she said, pulling him up so she could kiss him, taste the peppermint she remembered from the night she'd met Aiodhán. It made her think of Christmas, of finally being given everything she'd ever wanted, but nothing money or a title could buy. "Please, Aiodhán. I want you inside me."

His eyes were stormy gray with shiny blue flecks, like the summer Mediterranean waters she'd played in as a child. Only this particular delight was for her and her alone, and she didn't have her meddlesome parents telling her to be careful since she was the sole heir to the throne. She'd gladly drown in Aiodhán's liquid depths.

Without moving from his perch atop her hips, he tore off his scrub bottoms and looked at the bedside table.

"We don't really need any more of those, do we?" she asked, her smile wide.

Aiodhán's matching smile was wicked. "I'm so happy that you're knocked up, Princess de Reyes."

She giggled and bit her bottom lip. This man sitting over her was so gloriously handsome, so divine a creature, both inside and out. Not to mention he was a superb lover, one like she'd only imagined on her loneliest nights in her palace bedroom. And he was to be her *husband*.

If only she could expect this kind of happiness for the rest of her life. A deep worry lived beneath the joy she felt around him; she'd seen what her lifestyle demanded of people. Her father might not recall, but Luis had been decent once. In her opinion, he'd succumbed to the pressure the monarchy put on anyone within its sphere. What would it turn Aiodhán into?

Right now she meant to enjoy every last second. She opened for Aiodhán, tangling her fingers in his hair as his tip nudged her core.

"You're sure?" he asked. She nodded and slid closer so his length was pressed firmly against her.

"So very sure."

With that assurance, he rocked into her, and she gasped.

"Are you okay? Are you hurt?"

She laughed. "No, darling. I'm fine. It just feels different now. Everything is sensitive." He tentatively shifted, and she released a small moan. "I'm very fine indeed."

"Well, then, let's make the most of this new sensation."

Dipping down to kiss her, teasing her mouth open with his tongue, Aiodhán didn't slow his gentle glide in and out of her. Each nerve ending, each cell in her body was on fire, brought on and quenched by Aiodhán, the father of the small life growing inside her. God, she was to be a mother, and this man, her equal partner in raising their child.

She wrapped her arms tight around Aiodhán's shoulders, drawing him closer to her in the hopes she could grant the gravity of her situation leave for an hour or two of pleasure and release. She laced her fingers together behind his head and deepened their kiss. His kisses ignited a part of her soul that worried she'd never know love or anything resembling passion, burning it to ashes.

His hands roved over her body like a surgeon searching for a cure. He filled and explored all of her, and yet the weighty knowledge her time with him was limited didn't dissipate. If anything, it made her hungrier, more desperate to see him satisfied.

Lifting her own hips, she moved against him

until he growled into her mouth with a hunger that matched her own.

"Emilia." He groaned as she cupped beneath his erection. "Goddamn, woman. You feel…so…good."

"Igualmente, cariño."

His back tightened, and Emilia ran her fingertips down the strong length of him while he shuddered against her. Her own release came seconds later, and she couldn't help the cry of ecstasy that exploded from her.

Aiodhán stayed inside her but rolled them both on their sides. Her hands continued to trail up and down his muscular back. Appreciation for all he offered her, all he was sacrificing on her behalf, flooded from her fingertips and the soft kisses she peppered his chest with.

"That was…" he said, tipping her chin up so her gaze could fuse with his, "that was fantastic."

He kissed her before she could respond, forcing her to swallow the words on the tip of her tongue, forbidden words of love and promise and other things that should remain unsaid.

"It was," she said eventually.

His smile softened, and his eyes grew serious.

"I'm not the most emotionally available man," he said. Where she would have teased him earlier, his eyes—serious and gazing at her with intensity— said she should just listen. He paused, taking a deep breath. When he cupped her cheek, it simultaneously calmed and worried her. What was he having trouble articulating? "But I like this."

"Me, too. Very much." More words left unsaid. But this was enough. For now. In some ways it was more than she'd ever imagined. Yet somehow, the taste of Aiodhán left her greedy for all of it—all of him. He winked and squeezed her butt affectionately.

She kissed him then, for the confidence he exuded in their shared passion, for sharing child-rearing with her, for the nickname he'd coined for their unborn child. She only hoped who she was and had to become to rule a country didn't scare him away.

"We'll have the eyes of an entire nation on us, watching to see if we slip up. When you marry me, you're marrying into the crown and all that comes with that. Aiodhán, you'll be the prince consort of Zephyranthes after Friday. I don't say this to scare you, but we need to practice radical honesty if this is going to work. If things get to be too much, you need to talk to me so I can mitigate the effects on you and the country."

His thumb brushed her cheek, and she could feel the tension in his muscles beneath her hand. Neither of them would even be considering this if she weren't pregnant.

He'd said it himself moments before they'd just made love. He was only here because they had a daughter to raise together. Moments before they'd discovered her pregnancy, he'd been cool and indifferent to her. It was too much to hope the change in his heart would stick.

"Yeah, I've been ignoring that little addendum, actually. It's a lot."

She nodded. "At least we won't need those NDAs. The whole world will know about our marriage now, so what will a few extra nurses' eyes on us matter?" She'd tried for airy and playful but came up dreadfully short of trite.

His smile looked pained, especially the way his brows scrunched together in the center of his forehead.

"Will there be paparazzi at the hospital?"

"And outside our home. But that's where Chance comes in. He'll put a team together to ensure our lives remain as uninterrupted as possible. He's good at what he does, Aiodhán."

Aiodhán sighed and slid away from her, rolling on his back. She'd scared him. It hadn't been her intention, but it was better he knew what to expect now, before they made promises to one another they couldn't keep. All they really owed anyone was to put their child first; the rest was icing on a pretty top-heavy cake that might not be able to withstand the stress awaiting them.

"I wish I had known. You know, that night."

"Who I was?"

His hands were folded behind his head as he gazed at the ceiling. He'd gone from pulling her tight against his body to giving them all the space he could without rolling off the bed.

"Yeah." He glanced at her but didn't shift his body.

"Would it have changed anything?" Anxiety crept across her skin as she awaited his answer.

"No," he finally answered. "It wouldn't have. Nothing could have kept me from you, Emilia. But I would have liked to know more about you, where you came from, and what made you tick. Before so much was on the line."

"I agree. I'd only been in the country a few hours when we met, and to be honest, meeting you wasn't part of my plan, either. Not after Luis. I needed time to heal before I thought about anyone else. I did hope to try some American things like whiskey and hamburgers, maybe even put a song on a jukebox like they do in the movies."

"Sleeping with a stranger is about as ordinary and American as you could get."

They both laughed, and Aiodhán finally turned back toward her.

"Do you mind if I ask what happened with Luis? I mean, how did a sleazy guy like that get past your defenses? Hell, your dad's."

She sighed. The question was a fair one. And she'd agreed on radical honesty. "I think he was a good man trapped in an impossible situation, and though he was vetted and cleared, that wasn't enough to ensure he was supported in his role. He took the easy way out, but it cost him a lot. He'll never be allowed in Zephyranthes again, and we learned a lot about how to support newcomers to the family."

"Hence the lessons?"

"Hence the lessons."

Her smile didn't reach her eyes.

"Have I been vetted and cleared?" he teased.

She smiled. "If you hadn't, you'd be living in a prison somewhere south of Morocco," she teased back.

"Touché. But seriously, I'm sorry that happened to you. You deserve better, and as prince consortium—"

"Prince consort," she corrected, laughing.

"Yes, as that, I won't ever take the easy way out." The laughter faded, but her heart thumped against her chest.

She bit her bottom lip and nodded. "Okay, then. But you have to promise me something, Aiodhán."

"Anything."

"I don't want you to stay with me under some outdated sense of chivalry. I've had enough of that for a lifetime. If it's just about the baby, I can care for her alone."

Aiodhán laced his fingers around the base of her head and pulled her gently into him. His lips met hers, and where their earlier kisses had been passionate and fueled with something akin to desirous kerosene, this one was tender. Emotion passed from his lips to hers, carrying with them a depth that both frightened and calmed Emilia.

When he broke away, she was breathless and overwhelmed.

"It might have started that way, but it feels like there's more now."

"It does."

"I'll talk to you, Emilia, and I promise I always will, but you can be damn sure I won't let anyone in your royal entourage out chivalry me."

She giggled but grew serious when he kissed her again.

"I don't know what I'm doing, marrying a princess," he whispered against her skin. His breath was warm on her chilled skin, but his words still sent a shiver rolling through her. "But I can assure you, I'll rise to the challenge. Because I want to do right by *you*, Emilia the doctor and amazing woman."

He'd acknowledged the one thing that had been missing this whole time—that she was a woman affected by this decision, too, not just a womb for the infant princess.

"Oh, Aiodhán. I'm sorry for how this has all happened. But I'm grateful that it's you by my side."

"I'm not sorry. Even though it isn't what I thought my first go-around leading residents would look like, I'm glad that it happened."

Her giggle turned to a throaty laugh. "Give it time, Aiodhán. Give it time."

As he rolled on top of her, promising to make the most of the time they had before the crown pulled them for yet another press engagement by kissing her into submission, a small bead of hope rose to the surface of her thoughts.

If only she could ignore the world waiting just outside their door, ready to pounce on that hope and extinguish it in the name of curiosity.

CHAPTER THIRTEEN

AIODHÁN HAD BEEN out of the office for less than seventy-two hours, but it was still the longest stretch he'd gone without checking in or going through his emails at least. Stranger still was the fact that he didn't mind one damn bit. Instead of the steady thrum of noise in the back of his head urging him to work harder, to accomplish more, there was a peaceful silence.

The silence came with an almost magnetic pull toward Emilia, who quickly became his new obsession. If he wasn't making her comfortable after their press junkets, he was elevating her heartbeat with a passion-filled bout in her oversize bed. When he wasn't concerned about her food intake, he was licking chocolate sauce off her slightly swollen abdomen and trailing kisses south to an even sweeter spot. When he'd finished making sure the tiny life inside her was safe and healthy, he moved beside a sleeping Emilia and daydreamed about playing with a fake stethoscope with their little one, teaching them how to use the instrument.

Only once did he use his phone the whole weekend, and it was to work on something he figured they'd both need.

It was pretty easy to figure out—he was *happy*, and for maybe the first time in his life. If this was the payoff for the existential dread that plagued him each time he stepped away from her, he didn't mind.

When his alarm rang on the third morning away from the hospital, he almost hit Snooze to convince Emilia to wake him up in a far more sensual way than his coffee could. But she looked so peaceful, her eyes fluttering with dreams that must be good, given the sweet smile on her slightly parted lips.

Was he part of those dreams like she was in his? An ache to know the answer to that was as strong as his excitement to get back to the ER. He wasn't thrilled to go to work for the same reasons as before—to work away the loss that threatened to fill the cavernous spaces in his heart—but because he had a family to take care of now. A family that was filling those dark spaces with light.

He'd sworn to do what it took, and hell, if they could get off work and be together like they were the past few days, it would hardly be an imposition.

And in a few short hours, Emilia would be joining him at the hospital. He hopped out of bed, careful to shut the bathroom door quietly behind him.

It's going to be okay.

They'd already filled out all the HR forms and let the CMO know the plan, and he'd filled Mallory and Brian in. They were made aware of the minimum they needed to know, but it'd still been a surprise to hear Aiodhán had fallen for an intern, was marrying her in less than two weeks, and that she was a member of the royal Zephyr family. Oh, and he was gonna be a dad. Mallory had cried with happiness, and Brian had just sat there at the bar, his mouth agape, shaking his head.

"I can't believe it," his best friend repeated at least a dozen times in as many minutes. "You're actually gonna put a ring on her finger? Willingly?"

"I am."

He'd paid the tab and headed home, the smile remaining as he considered that word—*home*. Since the age of eleven he'd never really had one he looked forward to going to.

Brushing his teeth and heading out the door to the penthouse elevator, he contemplated his luck. It'd seemed like he'd stepped in some alternate universe when Emilia had strode through Minnie Gen's doors that first morning and he'd been forced to reckon with their one night of abandon every time he looked at her. But now he saw the fated second meeting for what it was: a portent of a future he was finally looking forward to. A future that would sustain him long after his career in medicine ended.

Emilia de Reyes was a gift he didn't plan on squandering.

When the doors opened in the lobby of the downtown apartment high-rise, though, he struggled to keep his focus. Flashing lights and a frenetic mob of people with cameras and microphones charged the doors. The noise was deafening, made worse by the way they charged him, bringing the chaos to his feet. Aiodhán glanced behind him as they approached, until it hit him.

They were there for *him*. The man about to marry Princess Emilia of Zephyranthes.

"Dr. Adler!" one reporter shouted from the back of the mob. "Is it true you're engaged to the princess?"

He ran through his talking points from the press secretary assigned to him and Emilia.

"Be brief. No details. Just good old-fashioned love that couldn't keep you two apart."

"I am. We're happy, and I'm sure she'll be willing to share more details soon, but if you'll excuse me, I'm late for work."

He pushed through the first membrane of reporters, surprised to find they were at least ten deep. Chance was shoving through on the other end, trying to make his way to Aiodhán, but the throng was relentless.

"How did you two meet?" another asked. He pretended he hadn't heard that one. Bar hopping and one-night stands were on the Do Not Mention list from the royal staff.

"Is it really love? How can you be sure when you've only known each other four months?"

"Were you aware she was one of the wealthiest people on the continent when you started dating? Do you think she'll ask you to sign a prenup after the fiasco with Luis Cartel?"

He used his shoulder to get through two more layers of the human shield blocking his way, refusing to answer the asinine questions from people who really didn't care about the answers.

Obviously there weren't prenuptial agreements in a royal marriage. He'd leave with nothing if he left, save a small stipend for his supposed troubles. He'd learned that much with an internet search. What happened to responsible journalism?

"Does this mean you'll be keeping up your medical practice? What about the proposed trauma center?"

Aiodhán frowned and turned to face the reporter who'd asked the last question. "Of course I'll keep practicing and building the center. Why wouldn't I?"

In the back of his head, he heard Florence, the press secretary's voice in his head.

"Don't get defensive. They'll try to rile you up, but don't let them."

"Will Princess Emilia stay on as an intern now that she's expecting?"

"You'll have to ask the princess." He tried for a smile, but damn if it didn't feel more like a grimace. A microphone was shoved in his face, actually slapping his chin when the reporter holding it was pushed from behind. Apologies were made, but the crowd didn't thin to make room for him to get to his car. How did Emilia do this every day of her life? No wonder she wanted a life of anonymity in America. One all her own without any prying eyes.

So much for that.

Chance finally broke through and snatched Aiodhán's hand.

"That's all the doctor has time for today. Please give him and the princess a wide berth so they can continue their lives without interruption," Chance said. It seemed to work, at least enough that Aiodhán could dive into the waiting car, Chance at his heels, before they sped off.

"Wow. That was intense." Aiodhán gazed out of the tinted window as the world he knew—usually by bike or on foot—whizzed by. He got the distinct feeling he was a bystander in his own life, a nagging tic that had flicked him upside the head from time to time since he'd found out about the pregnancy.

"Was it? That was a smaller gathering than we anticipated, actually. This makes me concerned the real crowd is awaiting our arrival at the hospital."

The *real* crowd? Hell. All he wanted at that moment was Emilia's hand in his so he could make his way to work unscathed. She gave him strength, and without her, he was floundering. So much for *I'll act like the royal consort I'm supposed to be.*

Maybe closer to the truth was *Please be easy on me. I just want to work and then go home to the woman I've agreed to marry and care for.*

Only one thing held him up. The reporters mentioned love more than once.

How would I answer that?

It wasn't that he didn't feel strongly for Emilia. But love? That was a different animal altogether. On one hand, he couldn't imagine life without her at his side now. But on the other hand, he'd never let anyone in, beyond mild attraction. How did he know what love felt like? Or could withstand? He was giving up his dream of the trauma center and helping more people to follow Emilia to her country. Was that love?

It'd been easy to imagine it was when he was tangled in Emilia's arms. Outside, faced with the only world he'd ever known—one he'd built from scratch—the answer was more difficult.

Chance passed him a single sheet of paper with a list of times and places he was needed for appearances, distracting him from the give-and-take of emotions surrounding his new circumstances.

"You're kidding me." His skin went cold. "What if I've got surgeries scheduled during these times?"

Chance shrugged. "I'm only the messenger, Dr. Adler."

"How many times do I have to beg you to call me Aiodhán?"

"At least one more, sir." Chance smiled, his eyes twinkling with mischief. A small bit of the frustration dissolved. This wasn't Chance's fault any more than it was his. Hell, if anyone was scot-free in the whole mess, it was Emilia's guard.

"Is this what we can expect every day this week leading up to the wedding?" Aiodhán asked him. "I just mean with these events and stuff. I'd like to know how important it is so I can keep the surgeries and resident duties I need in order to keep the program running. Not to mention get the work done at the trauma wing that's overdue at this point."

Anxiety crept up his spine.

"I think that is something you should speak with the king about."

And just like that, the frustration reappeared.

"Sure. Easy for you to say, since you're carrying a weapon under that seersucker." Aiodhán rolled his eyes at the window, at the brisk walk he was missing because he wasn't allowed to, as Florence, doubling as his household manager, said, "take unnecessary risks." So he couldn't walk, couldn't ride his bike, couldn't know why he was being pulled off surgeries and other duties for his job, but he could shut his mouth and go along with the status quo.

Maybe he should have asked more questions when Emilia said there would be challenges to being the prince consort. The thing was, he had. And she'd been nothing but honest. He just hadn't wanted to believe his life would so irrevocably altered.

Or perhaps he'd just imagined it to be like in the movies: princess meets prince, they fall in love, and everything falls into place. Instead, it was like watching a bomb go off in his life, and he was surgically trying to piece together what he could.

"This gets easier, you know," Chance said, by way of an answer to Aiodhán's childish outburst.

Aiodhán sighed, his breath fogging the glass. He absently traced the outline of the stop sign they were parked by. The octagonal red warning was clear. He needed to knock it off. He'd made every choice that had led to that moment. And it wouldn't last forever.

"Sorry about my attitude. I knew what to expect, but I guess I wasn't prepared for what it would feel like."

"How is that, sir?"

"Like I'm not in control of anything happening to me. Between the reporters and the schedule changes for the wedding, I'm not sure I'm in charge of my life anymore. I want Emilia and the baby, but I wish the rest of it wasn't part of the deal."

"That will pass with time. You'll get used to it, and choices will be made available to you so it doesn't seem as if this life isn't yours. In fact, I have a few of them here."

Chance handed him another piece of paper. Aiodhán opened it, and sure enough, there were a list of possibilities laid out for him.

He could marry Emilia and move to Zephyranthes with her, where he could take on a role as adviser of medical policy, which sounded made up. It sounded like a lot of travel and not a lot of time with his wife and daughter.

The next option was worse. He could stay here "for a number of predecided years" to continue his practice and supporting his family. On one hand, that didn't sound half-bad. His life would largely stay uninterrupted, and he'd get to visit Emilia and his daughter whenever he could.

Nowhere did it say he could move, practice medicine in Zephyranthes, and come home to his family each night. Did Emilia know about this?

The choices they'd given him were only okay if he'd remained the same man he'd been the night he'd met her. Now, he was somewhere between the idiot who pushed everyone away and the prince he'd need to become.

Where did that leave him?

Somewhere in the middle of the Atlantic Ocean.

"You don't have to go with one of those options, you know. You've usurped the royal lineage, so you hold more power than you think."

Aiodhán let that sink in. Chance was probably breaking three laws by mentioning that, but Aiodhán was only more confused than ever.

"I'm not going to blackmail them, Chance." He smiled. "But thanks for the talk. I'll work it out with Emilia."

He frowned at the crowd outside the hospital.

Aiodhán was a celebrity now, and everyone knew celebrities didn't get to keep the lives they left behind before they made the choice to step into the spotlight.

CHAPTER FOURTEEN

EMILIA GOT TO work without too much fuss. Of course, she'd been accosted by the gang of news folks outside the apartment and hospital, but that was to be expected. The questions were, too.

How long had she known the doctor?
Had they begun dating right after meeting?
What about Luis Cartel? Did he know?
Was it love at first sight?

That last one had given her pause, though she'd kept smiling, waving, and walking to the employee entrance of the ER as if nothing was amiss. On the surface, nothing was. She needn't think too hard on the attraction-at-first-sight aspect of her relationship with Aiodhán, but one word in that query had her heart aflutter.

Love. She'd never considered it possible, but here she was, living with a man she was to marry, a man whose baby she carried, and oh, it was everything she'd read about in the romance novels she'd stolen from her tutor's handbag when she was a young teen.

There was plenty of physical passion as she'd seen on the risqué pages of the romances she'd read, but there was also so much more. Aiodhán listened to her, and he took her ideas into consideration and built upon them. He laughed with her, and more than that, he invited her silliness.

It was just what she needed to face down the intense scrutiny awaiting her. Not from the cameras and writers attached to them; no, she could handle them as she had her whole life. But the peers she'd come to respect at the hospital were a different story. They wouldn't ever look at her the same way now that her true identity had been revealed. That, and the added judgment now that she was dating the boss. Would every good thing she'd done at the hospital be thrown into new light? Would they wonder if she received special treatment during her internship?

She knew how hard she'd worked, that they'd done everything above board, but still...worry tickled her skin.

"Are you sure you're ready for this, Emilia?" Rebecca asked her as the car came to a stop.

"I am. I've missed it here."

She felt stronger than she had since she'd arrived in Minnesota. Days of rest and good food and love-making could do that, she surmised.

"May I ask you a question?"

Emilia braced herself. She'd been waiting for Rebecca to come to her about the pregnancy instead of addressing the woman's own infertility trauma before she was ready.

"Of course."

"How did you muster the courage to chase this dream? Medicine, I mean."

Emilia was rarely surprised. Yet this question from Rebecca shocked her.

"Um... I'm not sure," she finally said. "I've wanted this life for as long as I could remember."

"Yes, I remember you trying to treat me for fatigue when I'd gone on a long ride through the Cyan fields."

Emilia laughed. "Didn't I prescribe you mints to take with every meal for a week after that?"

Rebecca offered a rare smile. "That you did. But what gave you the courage to pursue medicine as your passion project? Most nobles choose something like cooking in Italy or teaching in Africa."

"My mom." Rebecca's smile fell. "I'm sorry if that was blunt, but it's true. The woman may not have been who I thought she was, but her death affected me on a cellular level."

Rebecca gestured that Emilia continue.

"I didn't want anything to ever happen to anyone like what happened to my mother. When she asked for help, her doctors dismissed her as exhausted from labor—and she was a *queen*. By the time they realized she was bleeding internally, my brother had died in utero and my mother not long after. When I learned of the horrible conditions for women giving birth all over the world, my heart ached. I decided then and there I wouldn't let anything be more important than reaching that goal." Emilia got out and Rebecca sat in the car doorway. Reporters off in the distance hadn't noticed them yet, but their time was borrowed. "What did you want to do, Rebecca?"

Rebecca had been in Emilia's life since she was eleven. Only a year after Emilia's mother was buried, Rebecca walked down the aisle into the king's arms. Though it'd been almost two decades and Rebecca was legally Emilia's stepmother, she'd stayed just beyond Emilia's reach her whole life. Rebecca was only fifteen years older than Emilia, but that wasn't the only reason for the distance. Emilia had always sensed a jealousy emanating from the woman even though she was queen. She felt it even stronger now.

"To be honest, I'm sad we couldn't conceive, mostly because I know you and your father wanted it so badly—both for different reasons, I'm sure. But I never imagined being a mother. When your father met me, I was in graduate school to become an artist. I don't know if you knew that. He visited the school to see how the funds he'd donated were being put to use. Then…" she paused, a sad smile on her face.

"My father fell in love with you, and your life changed forever the moment you noticed him back."

Rebecca nodded. "And I fell in love back. I don't regret that, Emilia." For the first time since Emilia had watched Rebecca take her mother's crown, a peaceful understanding passed between the two women. It also helped her understand Aiodhán's struggles on a deeper level.

"Thank you for supporting me, Rebecca. And there's still time for you, too. Especially now."

Rebecca smiled as Emilia walked away. Their odd exchange weighed down Emilia's steps as she walked into the hospital with Chance. All it took was the familiar hiss of the doors opening for her to remember her purpose. A broad smile tugged at her lips, and her shoulders straightened with the importance of finding her life's work and performing her tasks with joy. That included becoming a queen worthy of the title.

She slipped past the main entrance without drawing the attention of the paparazzi outside. She could only hope Aiodhán had been able to do the same. This life was going to be a difficult enough adjustment for him; battling the unnecessary demons that plagued her position would only make it worse.

"Well, holy hell. I wasn't sure you'd come back," a welcome voice chimed in the moment she entered the lobby.

"Oh, Bridget, I've missed you."

The woman grinned and enveloped her in a hug. Emilia warmed at the affection. She'd never had a friend, but the gesture seemed to indicate she did now.

"Seriously, when you texted you were on your way in, I didn't believe you. Why the Sam hell would you come back here when you could, I dunno, run Zephyranthes and its wineries? I'd be back on the beaches of Cyana already, with a glass of Rioja and a plate of tapas on my lap."

Emilia let loose a laugh not becoming of a princess. "What? And give up our fourteen-hour-long days, the mystery meat in the cafeteria, and the nurse who I'm pretty sure tangles our picc lines on purpose? I wouldn't dream of it."

Bridget slapped her on the shoulder and led her to the locker room. Emilia inhaled the cool air of the hospital's lobby. The citrus-and-soap scent so endemic to the space slipped around her waist like the arm of a good friend, familiar and welcome.

"Don't forget about those flattering scrubs they gave us," Bridget added, cackling over her humor.

"Hey there. Don't disparage the pale blue wonders that are going to keep my belly hidden from all your prying eyes the next few months. Oh, and Rioja is off the menu for the time being."

Bridget grew serious. "I can't believe you're actually going through with the wedding," she whispered when the doors opened and the other interns strode in.

"Of course I am. I don't really have a choice, do I?"

Bridget shrugged, then her trademark smile kicked up in one corner of her mouth, matching the gleam in her eyes.

"I guess not, but you'd better promise me a dish session about you-know-who," she said in a hushed whisper meant only for Emilia. "I can forgive you for not telling me who you were in the beginning, but keeping the fact that you slept with the hottest doctor in the Midwest a secret? That's criminal."

Heat crept up Emilia's neck and cheeks. She could feel others' eyes on her as she changed into her scrubs. But the mention of Aiodhán calmed her. He was her partner in this. They could handle the pressure of the job, so long as they supported one another.

"If you can keep those interns off my back, I'll tell you everything."

"You're on. What about tonight? A wine and sparkling nonalcoholic cider date to celebrate your return?"

Emilia cringed. "I'm sorry, I can't. Aiodhán and I have dinner with my parents and the governor."

"No worries. How about tomorrow?"

"A press engagement at City Hall. We're pretty booked out, but I could probably sneak out for coffee one morning this weekend."

Although, as she mentioned it, she frowned. If she recalled, they had brunch Saturday with the mayor of Minneapolis and a champagne breakfast—sparkling cider for her—with the Department of Health of Minnesota on Sunday to discuss maternal care foundations she'd like the crown to donate to, including the Gold Fleece program.

The door shoved open, and Aiodhán called in. "Interns, out here now. We've got a lot to catch up on, and you're slowing us down."

The heat on Emilia's cheeks turned to molten lava at the sound of his voice. Her stomach flipped, and the warmth fled south.

Bridget gave her a weak hug laced with disappointment. This wasn't how Emilia imagined her reunion with Bridget. But her duties had to come first.

"It's okay. We'll find time. Oh, hey. Did your man tell you he asked me to join him at the new trauma center in the peds wing?"

Emilia nodded, hoping the jealousy she felt rising up her throat with bile didn't show. She'd love to work with them both, but not at the expense of her reputation or Aiodhán's.

"It's exciting!"

"I'll keep you posted about how it's going. If you want to say screw those other interns and what they think, you could always join us, you know."

If only it was just the interns talking about her behind her back.

"Thanks." Emilia tried for a smile, but even forced it barely worked. She wasn't sure she'd wanted the trauma position with Aiodhán—until she found out she'd be able to work with the neonatal patients. Giving it up was another loss she'd mourned in the privacy of her own heart, another price levied for the life she was born into. She couldn't afford to have anyone question how she earned her experiences. Especially not when their opinions could derail Aiodhán's career. This was one thing she could control, and she would, for them both. "Good luck, Bridget, and thank you for being there even though this is hard."

"Of course. You're my girl, Em, no matter what you are to the rest of them."

Aiodhán nodded that Bridget leave the locker room with the other interns, and when they were alone, he took Emilia in his arms and embraced her tightly.

"God, I missed you."

"I was only an hour behind you."

"An hour too long," he teased. His phone chimed twice in quick succession.

"Do you need to get that?" she asked.

He shrugged her concern off and ignored his phone, a liability as a doctor.

"It's nothing. Just something I'm working on."

She regarded him through a sidelong glance. "Care to share?"

"Not yet. When the time is right." His smile took the edge off her worry, but not completely. When his phone made a different chime, his smile disappeared. "Maybe we should just run away and forget all this mess."

"What happened?" she asked, pulling back. His eyes were hard, his jaw set.

"Just what you warned me would happen. Did you see our schedule? All but one of my surgeries have been canceled. I'm barely able to squeeze in time across the street."

"Oh, no. I'm so sorry. I actually don't think we have the same schedule. You'll be needed for more fittings and instruction on protocol that I've been learning since I was a child. But I can talk to my parents if it's too much."

Aiodhán pulled back, and the cool air between them chilled where his heat had been.

"No. No, that's fine. I'll be okay." His lips brushed hers, but they were devoid of the affection they'd shared earlier. "Have a good day with Dr. Thomas. Are you sure you want to do this? You can stay on my service, hon."

"No, not if I want to make a name for myself. This is okay for now, if it means people will look at the medicine I practice and not think I'm good because I'm getting help from my fiancé."

"I could always tell them to shove off."

She smiled. "I don't need you to fight my battles for me, Aiodhán. This one I need to do on my own."

"I'll support what you choose. But let me know if Bob doesn't work out. There's other options, Emilia."

"It's fine. Good luck over there."

They'd each said they were fine in the span of a couple minutes, so why didn't Emilia believe it? Because she wasn't, not really. So much was changing. Though much of it was good, she used to find peace and stability in the routine of royal life. Now the uncertainty circling her future left her feeling untethered and tossed around a stormy sea.

Aiodhán walked out, leaving her very alone and very unsure of how to fix this. How could she keep her friendship with Bridget, her duty to her country, grow a tiny life inside her, work hard at her profession, *and* build a relationship with a man she truly cared about at the center of it all? A moment ago, she'd had everything she'd ever wanted, and yet it felt as if it were slipping from her grasp.

And no one was coming to save her. There was no other heir, no one else's shoulders on which to share the burden of her crown when it became too heavy.

As she grabbed her lab coat and found her way to her new boss, her heart hammered against her chest. *Something is going to have to give*, it whispered to her.

That she believed.

CHAPTER FIFTEEN

AIODHÁN FINISHED THE final stitch of the biopsy and lifted his gloved hands.

"Bridget, you may close."

"Really?" Bridget asked. "Far out. I'll do you proud, boss."

Aiodhán simply nodded and headed out of the OR, stripping the gloves and face mask off when he was out of the sterile field. He sighed, watching on as Bridget—a fully competent, if overenthusiastic doctor—sutured the wound. It was their first patient together, and the procedure had gone as well as he could have hoped.

In an ideal world, Aiodhán would be able to keep Emilia on as an intern, but with the added scrutiny from their upcoming shotgun wedding, he understood why she'd opted to train under another physician. He respected her for the decision, even if he didn't care what anyone else thought of them.

Damn if he didn't miss her, though. Not just the warmth of her body he'd come to crave at the end of each long day, or the way her kisses could transform from soft and tentative to hungry and feverish within seconds. Yeah, he ached for those when he wasn't around her to claim them—especially now that the only hospital time he had was building up the trauma center across the street from him—but more than that, he missed *her*.

The wit he'd somehow overlooked, ebbing just below her intelligent responses at the hospital.

The way she knew just what he'd need moments before he asked for it.

Her ability to lead the interns without so much as a nudge. She commanded with her quiet strength and charm, and everyone just sort of fell in to learn from her. If he was honest, they'd all gotten more from Emilia than they had from him in the past five months.

But something nagged at him. She'd alluded to not knowing about his schedule, so did that mean she hadn't been aware of the king's ultimatum, either? Was it a boilerplate deal—marry the pregnant princess and pick one of two half-lives?

His pager went off and it startled him.

Surgery room 2, vehicle collision.

A second page went off.

Patient is 22 weeks pregnant.

Fear roared like a forest fire in heavy winds. Only repeating "She's here in the hospital" to himself took the edge off.

Still, the worry didn't dissipate. It never had, not since meeting Emilia. It'd only gotten worse after she'd collapsed in his ER.

He should give this case to someone else. But who? He pulled up the sheet of paper with his schedule from the king. If he took this on, he'd be late for the cocktail hour he and Emilia were scheduled for.

Well, that was too damned bad. Saving lives trumped drinks with strangers any day of the week.

He pocketed the schedule and jogged down the hall to the surgery suites. Over the past few days, he'd grown used to being interrupted by Emilia's parents or their staff in the middle of his day, but this would make two surgeries in a row without being yanked out. He needed this. If for no other reason than to calm the part of him that relied on putting families back together for his own peace.

Aiodhán pushed open the doors and strode into the sterile corridor to wash his hands and stopped short.

"Hey there, gorgeous. What are you doing here?"

Emilia beamed at him as she turned off the water with her wrists and shook them off.

"Dr. Thomas was annoyed with me, I think. He got the page and sent me instead."

"What an idiot. You can still work with me, you know."

She shrugged, then gestured to the stainless steel washbasin that looked out over the sparkling new surgical suite. "This place is amazing, Aiodhán. I wish I could." Her voice was wistful and tugged at his heart. Was there a time when he hadn't known the lilt of her vowels, the way she placed her bottom teeth between her lips when she was reticent? Of course there was, but he couldn't remember, nor did he want to. As challenging as it all had been, with the schedule interruptions and worry about what would come next for them as a new couple, he appreciated every minute he got to spend with Emilia.

In fact, he kept looking for more, *craved* more.

As a physician, he understood the feverish draw of an addict to a drug. Emilia was his, and he wouldn't mind being a lifetime user of the high she gave him.

"I do, too. Someday, hopefully, it'll matter a lot less to people how you got your start. They'll realize you're amazing, and that'll be all that counts."

"I hope so. The gossip in Middle America is certainly not for the faint of heart. I heard a man in front of me at the salad bar in the cafeteria, who I've never met mind you, comment on *the royal princess who was only hired to make the hospital look good*."

"Good grief. I'm sorry, Em." He was, too. He'd heard the rumors himself, but aside from telling the interns and other physicians to mind their own business, Emilia had asked him to stay out of it for fear of making things worse. He understood: the white-knighting wasn't going to help her show her own competence. Still, he wished there were more he could do besides stand by and support her decision. "You know the administration doesn't care. They know you're a good doctor and are fine with us sharing service. Just say the word, and I'll start pulling you over here until you're back to being mine."

"I'd like being yours." Her frown dissolved into a soft, lip-biting smile.

"Ditto." Aiodhán shook his head, the fear and worry fading like mist under a strong summer sun. "Well, I for one am glad Thomas is an insufferable tool who doesn't know greatness when he sees it. His loss is definitely my gain."

"You're sweet, but I'm not sure how I'm going to win his favor back."

"How so?"

Emilia bit the corner of her mouth in a way that made him half-hard and filled with the roaring desire that took over his good sense whenever he was with her. He threw on the cold water, hoping it would shock his system into remembering why he was there.

"He doesn't seem interested in instruction of, as he puts it, *a stuffed-shirt royal who won't be here long anyway.*"

"I know you want me to stay out of it, but when we're done here, I'm giving that jerk a piece of my mind. He has no right—"

"You'll do no such thing, Aiodhán Conor Adler. I can fight my own battles, thank you very much."

"And I love you for it." As soon as the words came out of his mouth, they both froze. Mortification spread from his toes to the tips of his ears as fast as a forest blaze in the middle of summer. Thankfully, she shook her head at his idiotic, purely unromantic way of telling her he loved her for the first time. "Sorry. That sure as hell isn't how I meant to tell you how I felt, but…"

He shrugged, his hands out in front of him, drying. When he bent in for a kiss, she met him halfway. The heat passing between them seared his feelings for her, capturing them in his heart.

"Well, I love you, too. But maybe we can talk about it after we're done saving lives and planning to overthrow the Zephyr monarchy with our unconventional marriage?"

Ask her about the letter from the king, his subconscious said.

No. Not right now. There was time.

"I'd like that."

"Dr. Adler, we could use you in here," the nurse came out to tell him. He nodded, pulled his mask over his face and hid his smile.

That is, until the phone buzzed in his pocket—the phone he'd been instructed to keep for de Reyes family communication. He let it buzz until curiosity finally got the best of him. Knowing he'd have to rewash his hands, he extracted the phone and read the stream of texts that followed.

There is a mandatory meeting at City Hall at three p.m. Please bring all documentation needed to procure a new passport, as well as your out-of-date items.

He frowned. They were making him renew his passport?

Of course, dummy. How else are you supposed to get to Zephyranthes to see your new wife?

It was two o'clock now. He wouldn't make it. Oh, well. Saving this woman—and her child's—life mattered more than some appointment that could be made up.

"What is it?" Emilia asked. "Is it my family?"

"Yeah, but it's not a big deal."

Wasn't it, though? Because this was the first step in his move to Zephyranthes someday so he could marry a woman who'd eventually rule a place he'd never even visited. His stomach hardened like it had been lined with lead.

"Talk to me, Aiodhán. Remember our radical honesty promise?"

He sighed. If he told her about every reservation he had, they'd never move past it. Some of the issues he had to work through on his own if he wanted to be the kind of partner Emilia deserved. The prince consort her country needed.

"I'm sorry, that's not what I was doing." He re-washed his hands and slid gloves on them. "Your family's staff asked me to get to City Hall to renew my passport."

"I understand, and I'm sorry. To say they oper-ate with royal efficiency wouldn't be hyperbole. But after Friday, we don't need to move on their time-line. We'll ask to take things slow, to figure out what we'd like to do as a couple."

A bit of the weight in his abdomen loosened.

"Okay. I like that. And I'm sorry I let it all get me wound up. It's just a lot to think about."

"I know." She nudged him with her shoulder. "But we're doing it together, and whatever choices we make will benefit our growing family."

She was right: they had a kid to think of now. He needed to stop getting so hung up on the small things when that was obviously the most important.

"All right. Let's do this, de Reyes."

She gloved up and put her surgical mask up as well, then followed him into the suite.

It was brightly lit, the instruments gleaming. This was Aiodhán's pulpit, his sanctuary, his Eden. Every patient he brought back helped smooth over the scar of a life interrupted. His life and childhood.

It might never be enough, but he had to try, right? At least this way, he put a little good in the world. Would he be able to say the same if he became the prince of another country, more or less a figurehead?

"Are you okay?" Emilia asked.

Aiodhán stood over the patient, the life in front of him heavy and difficult to imagine. Who was she, and more importantly, who was waiting on her to come home?

It hadn't occurred to Aiodhán to care much about those details. His job was to eviscerate unwanted illnesses and foreign objects, then suture together a new future for whomever ended up on his table. Who they were when they left wasn't ever his concern.

So why wouldn't his brain let that go just then?

It was Emilia.

If anything happened to her or their child she carried, he'd be the person in the hospital waiting room, desperate for her safety, for a second chance. She'd changed his motivations for working, living, and dreaming, and damn if that ripple effect didn't change the way he worked in his OR.

But was it enough to negate the after-effects of the texts still buzzing in his pocket since he'd ignored the first? To learn a new language, a new way of living, and all but give up medicine in the process?

He cleared his throat. He was working on at least one of those concerns, but it was slow going, reminding him of the noose tightening around his neck. *Time.* He was running out of time, and all the little unimportant engagements tugging at his schedule were removing the slack in the rope, cutting into his skin and plans.

"I'm fine. Let's get to work. Number five scalpel, please."

Emilia's gaze bore into Aiodhán, but he couldn't let it control the outcome in this room. She handed the instrument to him and grabbed the suction before he requested she do just that. His entire being was at war with itself. She made him better in so many ways, but she also made him vulnerable where he should be impermeable.

The patient had suffered injuries on the entire right side of her body, leading to a fractured rib, subdural hematoma, and a bleed he couldn't find.

An hour into cleaning the wound and searching for the cause of the destruction, Aiodhán shook his head in frustration.

"I can't find the bleeder," he said. His hands were deep in the patient's chest cavity, smeared with blood coming from a wound he couldn't see. The X-ray had shown the area, but it wasn't there. The infant's heart rate spiked. They were running out of time.

Emilia moved the suction, then followed the rib cage down with her hands. She mumbled in Zephyr and for the umpteenth time, he wished he'd paid more attention in his high school Spanish class. But he understood more than last time: that was something.

"I've looked there." The patient's heart rate slowed, while the baby's continued to rise, triggering both alarms. "I need more suction, de Reyes."

She used the suction wand while her other hand investigated, before announcing, "I've got it. There's trauma to the right kidney where it separated from the blood vessels. I've got my finger on the separation point. Should we suture?"

Aiodhán exhaled a breath he hadn't realized he'd kept locked in his chest.

"Good job, de Reyes. How big is the tear?"

"Enough that the bleed is consistent."

"Let's cauterize what we can then suture the vessel once she's out of immediate danger."

"Can I take lead?" she asked.

Aiodhán shivered as if a chill had draped over the room. When she'd stepped back, he could see the swelling of her abdomen. The only thing preventing her from ending up on this table was sheer luck. Being a royal didn't protect her, or them. And he was willingly signing up to care for this woman and this child, knowing he'd never know a day's peace again.

Yeah, but you're together for other reasons now.

Were they, though? His thoughts spiraled out of control quicker than he could rein them in.

"Aiodhán?" she asked. "I'm taking the lead." He

nodded and watched on as she asked the nurse for the cautery pen. In minutes, she was done and requested the sutures necessary to perform the vascular surgery. He assisted, but other than talking her through the closing, he hadn't done a damned thing.

The patient was wheeled to the recovery room, and Emilia wheeled on him.

"What was that, Aiodhán? You looked at me, at my stomach, and froze."

"I wasn't sure you could be objective." He nodded to her belly, housing the thing that brought them together in the first place.

"You have to trust that I'm going to be able to do this."

"I trust you, but this woman didn't end up in here of her own accord. The world's a scary place, and seeing her on the table made me think of you there. How do you separate it?"

She rested a hand on her abdomen. "If I let myself worry about our similarities, I wouldn't be able to do my job. And I'm training for neonatal surgery, Aiodhán."

"Should you be? I mean the stress of the baby with everything else going on—"

She froze, her bloodied hands held in front of her chest like a macabre offering.

"Is this about me or you right now?"

He ignored the sharp look from the anesthetist as she and the nurses left the room.

"Me. I get that, but this patient, Emilia… I can't protect you." There it was, his greatest fear laid on the table between them. "I mean, I can save all the lives in the world, but does it matter if I can't save you when it counts?"

She walked around the OR table to his side, dragging him out of the OR into the scrub room.

"You can't, you're right. Luckily, I can take care of myself. You're my partner, but it's not your job to save me. Nor is this a zero-sum game."

"How do you mean?"

"I mean, if you save a thousand people, it isn't bringing your parents back. And it won't protect anyone you love from harm."

She was right. He'd been racing the clock, trying to keep his heart safe while he protected other families. But that didn't change how he felt or why he'd avoided caring for anyone until now.

"It's just that… What about our child? When I'm a royal medical adviser, who's going to help keep her safe?"

Because even if Emilia could take care of herself, who would protect their daughter when he was working in some job he didn't understand on behalf of a country that wasn't his?

Shock registered in her wide eyes before her brows crashed together in a small act of fury.

"What the hell are you talking about? That's not even a real thing, Aiodhán. If you don't want to marry me and move, just—"

He'd stripped his gloves and tore out the letter that had been burning a hole in his shirt pocket.

"Then, what's this?"

She stripped her own gloves, and he watched her eyes widen with every line of the letter from her father.

"I—I don't know. But they must have a plan for you if that's what they came up with. Most likely it's a way to get you medical privileges without you having to be credentialed in Zephyranthes."

The naked truth of her statement fell on him like a thousand tiny paper cuts, stinging him but leaving him open and burning. Her parents had made up a position to pacify him, so not only was he losing his homeland, his friends, and freedom but he'd lose his practice as well. Unless he stayed here, which, he recalled, was their second option. Or was it their first? Were they hoping he'd take the easier route and they wouldn't have to come up with a job description for the royal medical something-or-other?

"Oh."

"Don't worry about it right now. We'll get it sorted."

Her dismissal was salt in his wounds.

"Sure. I'm sure it's going to work out."

"It has to," she whispered.

He pulled her into him and closed his eyes. This was his partner, the woman he'd just admitted loving and who carried his child inside her. She was struggling, too, despite being strong so much of the time—strong enough to carry him through his worry, too. He could do this. He had to, for her.

But would it be enough?

When he secured his arms around Emilia in a

viselike grip, it was for himself. Maybe, if he held on tight enough, he could keep the outside world from taking what he loved this time around.

The door cracked open, and Bridget stuck her head in.

"Hey, you two. I've been waiting out here until you finish up, but since it looks like you're moving in here for the night, I figured I'd just interrupt."

"What's going on, Bridget?" Emilia asked.

"Your parents are in the lobby."

Aiodhán cringed. Shoot. He'd forgotten about his appointment with them.

"Why didn't they call me?"

"They're not here for you," she said. "I guess they had some sort of meeting with you, Dr. Adler. You're two hours late, they said."

"What's this about?" Emilia asked him. "And why didn't you say anything? I could have paged another doctor."

"Who? Who could have done what I did back there, Emi?" He raked his hands through his hair as Bridget slipped from the room.

"You can't play God like this, Aiodhán. You're a fabulous physician, but you're not the only one here."

"That's not the point."

Her hands rested on her hips. God, he both loved and despised when she did that. It was sexy as hell but usually meant she was pissed at him.

"Then what, pray tell, is?"

"Do you see what's happening? I love what I do, Emilia, and they're taking it from me."

"It'll only be—"

"For a few more days. I know." He shoved out of the doors, leaving Emilia behind in the scrub room. It wasn't right to take this out on her, he knew. But he was powerless to stop the royal wheel that was already in motion. Even though it was rolling right over his dreams and career.

"Aiodhán, look at me." He did and saw the hurt in her eyes. He wasn't the only one giving things up in this exchange.

He kissed the top of her head. "I'm sorry. I'm frustrated—"

"No. No apologies. But no wallowing, either."

"What's the alternative?" he said, only half-teasing.

"You find a way to get what you want out of this spin on your life, so you don't feel as steamrolled."

He considered that. What did he want? Besides the woman already in his arms, that is. And there was his answer. He'd been selfishly thinking about what he was losing if he married Emilia, but not how she must be feeling in all the upheaval. Hell, the woman had given up her position on his service to protect them both.

"Okay, hon. I can do that."

He changed out quickly, the sleek black suit and slicked back hair uncomfortable but necessary.

The pager buzzed again, and he wished he could chuck it at the door. The hospital would have to find someone else to perform the surgery: Aiodhán could no longer afford to ignore the king and queen. A whisper of an idea—an idea that had been nagging him—fluttered around in his head as he strode toward the lobby.

No, he didn't want to keep his future in-laws waiting, not when they had the power to help him out with a project he'd been thinking about. Maybe it was time to use this relationship to get something *he* wanted for a change.

CHAPTER SIXTEEN

EMILIA CHECKED HER TABLET. Only two more patients left on her rounds. Both were OB patients, which sent a thrill of excitement coursing through her veins. This was what she'd come to America for, what she'd pushed back her familial and royal obligations to do.

She stopped at the first room to find the patient sleeping. It always bothered her to rouse patients who clearly needed rest, but that was the job. As was working with men like Bob Thomas. Emilia shuddered, even though she hadn't laid eyes on the man in almost two hours.

"How is he?" Bridget had asked her at lunch on Emilia's third day back. "I've heard he's like the troll from the kids' story, guarding his patients like the troll guarded his bridge."

"Dr. Thomas is brilliant, and I'll learn a lot from him," Emilia replied, her practiced response.

Liar. You actually called him a jealous troll under your breath after he took credit for your last save.

Bridget had eyed her suspiciously, and for good reason. Emilia found it hard to complain when she'd put herself in this situation. But regaining her reputation as a top-notch intern had been more important at the time than working with him. Now, she wasn't sure that choice had been worth it.

"Ew… Like that's the point." Emilia had laughed

at how different she and her friend were. "I'm just saying, you'd better learn enough to graduate early. Because Dr. Thomas isn't a quarter as good-looking as your last boss," Bridget had teased before snatching an olive from Emilia's salad. She didn't mind; she hadn't had much of an appetite the past few days. And of course her friend would bring up Aiodhán. As if Emilia could put him from her mind for more than a moment.

Between her pregnancy and the impending wedding, Emilia was a bundle of nerves. Her focus was pulled between the two, and she still strove to learn and take in as much as she could before this was all taken from her.

But the truth was, she'd never become the type of surgeon she wanted to be by watching.

It was frustrating to be sure, and it made her appreciate the intensity of Aiodhán's first weeks of instruction. At least he'd acknowledged when she'd done something well or allowed her to correct her own mistakes.

Speaking of Aiodhán, and of his grumpiness, he'd become distant at work again. Not emotionally—no, he was as supportive as ever. But she hardly ever saw him anymore. Their lives had changed, and it was time she accepted that. It would only be truer after their daughter was born.

She'd asked him where he went at lunch or after his shift, and Aiodhán had said, "You're just going to have to trust me." The soft smile she'd received consoled her, but barely. She trusted him, of course, but she also missed him.

She'd just have to dive into the kisses and tender caresses of their nights together, to cherish what they were able to share when they were able to share it.

She'd yet to ask her parents about the advisory position they'd created for him. It was clear it was a fake position, a way to make him feel a part of something he might never fully acclimate to.

That small worry nagged at her, but aside from talking to her father, what could she do? She was at the mercy of royal protocol as much as Aiodhán was.

And yet…a matter of days remained until Aiodhán became her husband. Then, her parents would return to Zephyranthes until the birth, and she and Aiodhán could go back to concentrating on their shared love of medicine. There was a world of time to plan the future beyond that.

"Good morning, Mrs. Reynolds. How did you sleep?" Emilia asked as she entered her last patient's room. She checked the chart at the end of the bed as well as the monitors, and her mouth twisted into a frown. She'd feel more confident if Mrs. Reynolds's numbers were a little better. She was only two centimeters dilated and thirty percent effaced, but her heart rate and that of her infant were a tad high for Emilia's liking.

"Okay, thanks. I'd have slept better if I could convince Sarah to come out a little early."

"Did you decide on Sarah, then?"

Mrs. Reynolds laughed, then winced, holding her

belly. "I'm just trying it out. Mark likes it since it was his great-aunt's name, but I'm not sure."

"Okay. What are some of your other choices?"

While Mrs. Reynolds told her the other names topping their list for the baby, Emilia discreetly paged Aiodhán. The OB attending was with another patient, and Dr. Thomas was out for the afternoon at a seminar, which left all the interns under the purview of her future husband. Less than a minute later, he strode through the door as Mrs. Reynolds shared the final name on her list.

"If I had my way, I'd go with Eleanor. That was my mother's name and could be shortened to Ellie or Elle."

"My mother's name was Eleanor, too," Aiodhán said. Emilia's curiosity was piqued. She hadn't known that about Aiodhán's mother. The list was so long about what they didn't know, at times it overwhelmed her. "I'm Dr. Adler, the doc on call today, Mrs. Reynolds. It's nice to meet you."

"Where is my OB? She knows I'm here and said she'd come by."

"She'll come by after surgery to take a peek at the baby." Mrs. Reynolds nodded, pacing her own breathing. But her skin was warm and damp, not a good sign. Aiodhán sent Emilia a knowing glance. "Dr. de Reyes just wanted me to take a look at things to make sure you're doing okay. How do you feel?"

"Mmm. Okay. Hot, I guess? Maybe a little dizzy."

"Okay. I'll see what I can do to help."

Emilia pointed out the numbers on the machine next to the patient. He frowned as well.

"Wow. Are all doctors as handsome as him?" Mrs. Reynolds whispered to Emilia.

"Not a single one. He's quite the charmer, too." She winked and tracked Mrs. Reynolds' smile. It was sharp, forced. They'd be meeting her daughter sooner than expected.

"Mrs. Reynolds," Aiodhán said, "I'm afraid I don't like what I'm seeing. I'd like to wheel you into surgery so we can make sure your daughter is delivered safely. It would be a lot better for both your hearts, which are pumping a little fast for me to recommend a natural birth."

The blood drained from her face. Her bottom lip quivered.

"But my husband isn't here yet," she whispered. Just then, another contraction rocketed through her, and she let out an ear-splitting groan before losing consciousness.

"We've got to move, Emilia. Now."

Emilia nodded and tore open the door for Aiodhán to push the gurney through. She raced behind him until they got to the OR suite in the maternity ward.

"I've called ahead to the anesthetist," she said as they slammed through the doors of the OR. "He'll be here soon."

"Good. See if you can find her husband. Fill him in, and then get back here to assist."

Emilia nodded, her nerves frayed, though she hid

it beneath the royal stoicism that had been bred into her and served her well. After turning the corner, sure she was out of sight of Aiodhán, she let her hands fall to her abdomen, the hint of the small human growing inside it swelling against her skin. Heat built behind her lids, but she would not let the tears fall. Mrs. Reynolds's story wasn't her mother's. It wasn't hers, either.

Though, the other day in the OR with the woman who'd been in the car accident, she'd felt the edge of fear sneaking up on her. It had been obvious Aiodhán was terrified, so she'd shoved the worry aside.

She didn't want to add more to his plate, though, so she'd hide it until the stress of the wedding was over. Besides, her pregnancy was normal so far, a miracle since she'd received no prenatal care before her sixteenth week.

That was the thing about pregnancy: it was such a seemingly similar, benign event that occurred to an impressive percentage of people who experience pregnancy at some point in their lives. Yet each one was like a fingerprint, unique and special.

She headed down the stairs to the lobby, keeping an eye out for the red-haired, tall man she'd seen in her patient's room before.

Worry plagued her as she scoured the bustle of faces milling about. Distinct births could mean unique complications. Her mother had died from internal bleeding no one caught, barely outliving a son. She'd collapsed much the same as Mrs. Reynolds and hadn't woken up again.

Emilia noticed she'd thought of her mother without going first to the betrayal of the woman. She was healing, largely due to Aiodhán's influence on her life.

A steady warmth flowed over and through her as she considered her husband-to-be. If she could have designed a more perfect match for herself, she didn't think she would be able to do better than the physician who'd stolen her heart. What would she change? Most certainly their circumstances. If left to their own devices, she had no doubt she and Aiodhán wouldn't have found their way to one another. Her pregnancy had brought them together, but it also brought the stress of the baby, the shotgun wedding, and the pressure to move to Zephyranthes…

It was a lot.

A flash of red dashed in front of Emilia, capturing her attention.

"Mr. Reynolds," she shouted across the lobby. The man stopped and turned in her direction. She sighed with relief as he walked toward her. "I'm a resident here at Minneapolis General, and your wife has been brought to surgery to have a C-section."

"Oh, my God. What—what happened?" he asked. "I just went to get her some thicker socks and figured I'd pick up this…" he choked on a sob "…this blanket for our little girl."

Emilia placed a hand on his arm. "Mr. Reynolds, we have the best team working to help your wife and daughter. I'll update you personally as we progress through the surgery, but you should know cesareans are common, even emergent ones such as your wife's. Hold onto that blanket—you'll be needing it soon."

"Thank you for coming to tell me. Should I wait here, or…"

Emilia shook her head, an idea forming. "No, come with me. You can sit in the gallery if you'd like to watch, or you can sit in the maternity lobby. She won't likely go back to her old room for a bit until we make sure she's stable enough."

"Okay. Yeah. I'll come watch."

Emilia led the way and showed Mr. Reynolds where he could watch the birth of his little girl before scrubbing in to join Aiodhán.

"Is he aware of his wife's condition?" Aiodhán asked as soon as she entered the sterile surgical field where Mrs. Reynolds lay, still unconscious but anesthetized as well.

"We've invited partners to watch the birth before," Emilia replied. "He's scared."

What she didn't say? *I'm scared. Please, let me control what I can.*

"I understand, and I'm not questioning your choice. I just want to be prepared. This is bad, Emilia." She'd thought of that, but she also imagined not being able to see Aiodhán in his last moments. Suddenly it was clear what had happened to her: like Aiodhán, she had something to lose, and that was unimaginable.

"What do you need me to do to support you here?" she asked. He glanced up, scalpel in hand.

His gaze brushed over her, but she didn't miss the way it lingered ever so slightly on the swelling of her abdomen.

"Exactly what you're doing." Emotion overwhelmed her; the baby had changed so much between them. "Help me assess the damage from her placenta abruption. She's bleeding, and I need to get it under control."

"It's placenta?" she asked, a slight wave of fear hitting her like a Mediterranean winter storm. Mrs. Reynolds's case and her mother's were more similar than she'd initially suspected.

"Yes. And it's severe. I'm a little pissed Dr. Young missed it, to be honest. It's not a mild case, and Mrs. Reynolds must've been presenting with symptoms this whole time. She was lucky to have had you on her service tonight, Emilia."

Was there an element of luck to what they did?

Emilia steeled herself, pulling strength from within. She owed the mother on the other side of the fabric her full attention. She stretched her fingers until the tremble abated. There was a reason she'd chosen this focus.

"She will get to meet Eleanor, and her husband will give them the baby blanket he picked out for her."

"Damn straight. Now, let's get to work."

As soon as the words were out of his mouth, Mrs. Reynolds coded, the long slow beep announcing her loss of sinus rhythm deafening.

"No way," Aiodhán muttered. "Not today."

He started chest compressions while Emilia performed CPR.

"Bag her, Emi. It'll be easier on your body." She nodded and worked the oxygen bag until the steady *beep-pause*, *beep-pause* returned.

"Whew. That was close. We've got to get that baby out and see what's tearing her up."

They moved together as one, suturing and clamping and suctioning until the bleeding stopped. They delivered the baby, who offered the world a blood-curdling scream. It was the best sound Emilia had ever heard. Especially when it was paired with the steady hum of the heart rate monitor. Mrs. Reynolds would be okay.

Emilia was the furthest thing from happy in that moment, but an infinitesimal bloom of hope blossomed in her heart. Aiodhán was wonderful. Giving and intelligent, kind and dedicated, handsome and humble.

Emilia took the baby to the incubator to be measured and checked out, but not before holding her up so her father could see her sweet, cherub face from the gallery. Tears streamed down his face, and Emilia felt her own tears dampening the inside of her mask. He mouthed *thank you*, and a crack as wide as the Pyrenees opened in her chest.

"That was a good save, Emi. You made your mark today and should be proud."

She was.

"Thank you, Aiodhán. I appreciate you being

there when Dr. Thomas leaves me behind. Especially when you're so exhausted."

"I'm always going to support your choices, Em." He bit his bottom lip and shook his head. "Even when I'm tired or frustrated. I love you. Already, despite your family or this job we've committed to… None of it matters. *I love you.* It just might come with some stuff I've got to work through."

Curiosity flirted with her.

"What stuff?"

He sighed and motioned to the scrub room where they'd be alone. She followed him out.

"I *am* exhausted, Emi. I'd rather work twenty-hour days saving lives than eight straight hours of the meetings and press releases and stuff they're pulling me for. I just…" He sighed as he ran the water over his hands while his gaze focused on something in the distance she couldn't see. "If I'm being honest, I don't know that I'm meant for this life, one split between medicine and…and politics. Have you had a chance to talk to your parents yet?"

"I haven't." She told herself it was because they had time, but the reality was deeper, darker. What if her family was complicit in taking Aiodhán's career from him? That made her complicit since she'd never do anything to get in the way of what was best for the crown. Was taking on a husband she loved part of that? Until her father had married Rebecca, no Zephyr monarch had married for love.

She knew then who she had to talk to, and hopefully it would solve two questions at the same time.

"I haven't, honestly. But I will today. I'll get our lives—and our careers—back."

His smile didn't meet his eyes.

"What else is bothering you?"

He paused before shaking his head.

"I'm just proud of you."

"What do you mean?" she asked.

He grasped her hand. "Those two women almost lost their lives, and their babies'. And their spouses? You can't imagine what it's like going from not caring about anyone to loving two people so completely your heart feels like it's walking around outside your body. I'm terrified all the time and you." He kissed her. "You're doing what you came here to do. It's amazing, Emilia. You make me a stronger doctor, even if I'm scared senseless every time I see a pregnant woman in the OR."

It was as if Emilia carried her own fear like a secret, even from Aiodhán. Aiodhán met her gaze, then looked up through the glass at their patient, who would be wheeled to the ICU until she recovered enough from the traumatic birth to be released.

"You're a brilliant doctor who makes the tough calls and seems unfazed."

She laughed, but it lacked any humor. It was time to tell him the truth. She was scared, too.

"I'm the furthest thing from unfazed, Aiodhán. My mother died from pregnancy complications. I was already hospitalized for my own, and I'm terrified that I'm dragging you into a world that might not hit you with a bus but kill you slowly over time."

He smiled. "Well, that's a relief. I'm glad we're together on that, but I meant what I said. In spite of it all, you're doing your job, and the hospital—and I—are better for it. Thank you."

She tucked herself into Aiodhán's arm. He squeezed her tight.

Aiodhán smiled and gazed down at her. "You can tell me, you know. When you're struggling. I won't rush to fix it, but I would like to know when I can be a shoulder to lean on. Radical honesty, Em."

"Radical honesty."

But before she could make good on that promise, there was a conversation she needed to have.

CHAPTER SEVENTEEN

EMILIA DIDN'T BELIEVE in regrets the same way she didn't believe in fate. Which was probably how she found herself in this position in the first place. She'd looked Lady Fate straight in her eyes and laughed at the bar the night she'd met Aiodhán thinking she was oh, so clever. Now, here she was, pregnant and alone since Aiodhán had taken on extra shifts the past two nights to make up for the cases he was pulled from during the day.

Try as she did to wait up for him both evenings, her will had succumbed to the needs of the tiny life growing inside her, and she never made it more than an episode into whatever police procedural she was watching.

She'd tried to talk to Rebecca about the letter they'd given Aiodhán, but her stepmother had been vague. It was boilerplate, just an outline to get them all thinking…blah, blah, blah.

Emilia didn't buy it, but she also had no brain cells left to figure out her parents' plan. On one hand, it seemed as if they were supportive of Emilia and Aiodhán, even going so far as to bring him into the security briefings they attended via remote server. On the other hand, Emilia felt as if she were being held behind a smoke screen.

She'd worry about it after work. Right now, she

needed to keep her pregnancy brain—and energy—focused on her job.

She yawned and tied the scrub cap tight against her head, tucking any errant hairs under the soft fabric patterned after her home country's flag. Bridget had bought it for her as an early bridesmaid gift, though Emilia was still a little foggy on the point of such a thing. Not the scrub cap, but the idea of having a celebration to mark the end of being, as Bridget put it, *single AF.*

As if she'd ever been single a day in her life. She'd been married to the crown, betrothed to an idea of a man who'd bring her country stability, even engaged at one point to someone they'd thought would fill that role.

But Emilia had never been single.

Which is why her relationship with Aiodhán was so peculiar. He'd not only upended her so-called dating status but her *life.*

Even though she loved him, could clearly see the new life laid out for them, if pressed she'd admit it wasn't what she'd hoped for when she came to America. Not even close.

"You ready for tonight?" Bridget asked, slamming open the locker room door. She glanced at Emilia and frowned. "You okay?"

Emilia sighed. "Sorry, I'm just a bit grumpy because I haven't seen my fiancé in days, it seems."

"Aww, you two are too cute. Well, I'm happy to distract you tonight so you don't get too lonely."

"Lonely? No, I'll be asleep. You made the party

after dinner, which is my new bedtime." They shared a laugh. "Can't we just call in a movie and wear comfy robes while someone rubs my feet?"

Emilia pasted on a cheesy grin, complete with pleading hands that looked close to begging or praying or something she wasn't above if it would get her out of this night.

Bridget laughed and hooked her arm in Emilia's. "Nice try. You're getting married Saturday, in America, so you're taking part in this ridiculous American tradition. You need this. You just don't know it yet."

"Oh, I need something," Emilia muttered under her breath as they left the room, tablets in hand.

"What was that?"

"Nothing. Let's get this set of rounds over with so I might sneak in a nap before you drag me across the city. You'd better let me wear my trainers, at least."

A couple hours and two tough cases that brought Emilia to her knees physically and emotionally, and the sight of Bridget strolling down the corridor toward her didn't bring with it the joy it normally did.

"So are you ready to par-tay?"

Emilia was decidedly *not*, but she put on her bravest face and nodded. This was important to her best friend, so she'd go along with it.

When they got in the car, Bridget had a soft smile on her face.

"What is that look you're wearing?" Emilia asked.

"What, my smile?"

"You're up to something…"

Bridget shrugged. "What if I am?"

If she was, and she wasn't mentioning it to Emilia, then it must be bad.

"If you make me so tired I look awful in my wedding photos Saturday, so help me…"

"You'll look fabulous. I promise."

Yeah, well, your promise couldn't hold up the weight of a feather, she wanted to tell her friend, who kept the mischievous grin on her face the duration of the ride to Emilia's apartment.

When they pulled up to the front, Emilia got out, and Bridget locked the car door behind her. She rolled down the window, though.

"Aren't you coming up with me to choose an outfit?" Emilia asked.

"Have fun tonight, and don't say I never gave you anything. Oh, and I'll be expecting the real thing when you have that kid, okay?"

With that, Bridget winked and zoomed out of the parking lot, leaving Emilia alone and terribly confused.

She parsed the last few minutes on her way up in the elevator, but when the doors opened to the penthouse, it all vanished in the breath she gasped out.

"What…what is this?" she asked Aiodhán. He held a bouquet of lilies—her favorites, and the national flower of her country—in his hands, but she hardly saw them when he took up all the space, all the air in the room. Bare chested, barefooted, and clad only in baggy gray sweats, he was the picture of comfort. If comfort was supposed to make one warm and tingly inside, that was.

"It's for you. All of it." He gestured to the sepulchral space that had been done up like the inside of a spa. "Well, for all three of us, actually." There were fresh lilies and hydrangeas on every surface, as well as Zephyr tapas beneath them. Emilia inhaled deeply; the floral aroma mixed with the spices of her country, a place she'd only recently come to miss. It undid a locked box in Emilia's chest, and the tears built quickly.

"It's beautiful," she said. "But what about Bridget? She has this whole evening planned for me."

"No," Aiodhán said, putting the flowers on the dining table and wrapping Emilia up in a hug that both calmed her and sent her heart racing at the same time. That was the power of the man she was to marry. "This is it. Her only job was to get you here so you could have a night of relaxation—so *we* could have a night to relax together. Do you like it?"

She nodded, and only then did Emilia notice there were three stations with people beside their setups.

Two masseurs were on hand with massage tables next to a woman with a pop-up nail salon, and another spot was tucked in the corner for hair. The strangers all dipped their eyes to the floor so as to give the couple some privacy. At least they would stop her from jumping her fiancé like she wanted to at that moment. Emilia wasn't sure if it was the pregnancy hormones or the man himself that made her crave him as she did. Probably a combination of them both.

"It's amazing, Aiodhán. How did you pull it off?"

"Very carefully and almost not at all when a few of our plans got waylaid by Zephyranthes and Minnie Gen."

"Zephyranthes?" Confusion swirled along with lust in her stomach, making it flip.

"Yeah. I had some help from your parents, but of course it had to happen between royal duties, which pulled them away a couple times. I've got to say, if the people there are as demanding as the king and queen, maybe it's better we're here."

He winked, drawing out a smile from her.

"My parents helped with this? I never imagined…"

"I didn't think so, either, but they just want you happy, Emi. They were so glad to take part in this night."

"I… I don't know what to say," she said. "Rebecca was so vague when I talked to her about your letter—"

"That's my fault. I addressed it with her when I asked about this, about the lilies and tapas."

"And?"

He shrugged. The light in his eyes dimmed ever so slightly, but his smile was fixed in place.

"It's a starting point. I can practice, but with the added security to the hospital over there, it might not be worth the hassle. We'll see."

"Oh, Aiodhán. I'm so sorry."

He waved her off. "It'll be okay. I promised to

take care of you and the bean, and that's what's most important. But enough about that. Tonight is about pampering *you*."

Her gaze fell on the massage table, and her hand went to her stomach. "Oh, I can't get a massage because of the preg—"

"She's a neonatal specialist. It's safe, I promise."

"Thank you for thinking about that. But what about the hair—won't that be ruined by Saturday?"

He cupped a hand along her cheek, tangling his fingers in her curls. God, how she'd missed his touch, his scent, his body… He softly kissed her lips before handing her a cerulean silk robe the same color as her wedding palette.

"The hair person is for Saturday morning so you don't have to go anywhere. She just wants to try a couple styles tonight so she knows what you want on the day." Tears sprung behind her eyes. Between her pregnancy, her internship, and Aiodhán's work, she'd barely had time to consider the smaller facets of her wedding day. And he'd done it all for her, even despite his hectic schedule.

"Is this where you've been in the evenings?"

"Sort of. I've actually been working since my days have been spent getting this together along with the growing to-do list from your parents. It's why I needed you to trust me when you asked about my late hours: I couldn't pull this off at home, with you lying on my chest. I wish I could have said something, but I wanted to give you something special and hoped it would be a surprise."

"It is, and it's lovely."

"I'm glad you like it. We took care of everything, Em. Change into this when you're ready, then just relax and enjoy." She smiled, biting her bottom lip. "Oh, but Bridget did say this gives her full access to you after you give birth. She's gonna want to do this night the good old-fashioned Southern way, she told me."

Emilia laughed, a heavy weight lifted from her shoulders. "That's fine. She told me as much, but I didn't understand why at the time. It makes sense now. But, Aiodhán?"

"Yeah?"

"Why… I mean, when? No, I guess I meant *why* as well."

Aiodhán chuckled.

"Because you deserve more from all of us. After my last meeting with your folks, I talked to them about my needs for the hospital and trauma center while we're here so I can leave it in good hands, but also for you. They can't keep pulling me from their daughter, or something was going to give. I told them I didn't want it to be you. You deserve everything, not scraps."

"I just can't believe how much you did. For me."

He pulled her into his chest. "For us. For our daughter. I know work has been running me ragged, but you have to know how much I care about our little bean. It's worth it to keep you both safe."

A small tinge of worry bubbled up amid the joy. He kept repeating his mantra—keeping her safe—

no matter how many times they talked about what was within their control and what wasn't. And it all came back to their bean.

Another worry bubbled up, this one always at the edge of her thoughts. What if this was just another version of fixing what had happened with the loss of his parents, another tally in his attempt to right the scales?

"Aiodhán," she whispered, "are you happy?"

His eyes narrowed, but he tried on a smile for her. It was a shadow of the one he'd worn when they met.

"I will be. I've got so much to be happy for."

A tremble of worry rumbled in her chest. There was a breaking point for this man, and mercifully, they hadn't discovered it yet. But they were close, and when it came, she was certain it would take her under, too.

There was only one way to prevent all of this, to save the man she loved from a life that was running him ragged and might take his career away from him…

From being miserable and pretending he wasn't.

She wished there wasn't a room full of people, that she could sit him down and tell him how she felt. After they left, perhaps?

I have to set him free.

He could support her and the baby, visit even. But going forward the way they were was untenable.

There has to be another way, her heart screamed.

She ignored it. Try as she might, she couldn't see any other possibility, not one that would protect

Aiodhán. Emilia was a princess; her life was never going to be her own. But the man she loved deeper than she'd ever dreamed possible?

She could—and would—save him from the same fate. Even if it cost her any chance at happiness.

Even if the heart she'd silenced broke into a thousand pieces.

CHAPTER EIGHTEEN

AIODHÁN SLEPT WELL for the first night in who knew how long. Actually, he knew exactly how long it'd been since he'd hit the pillow and crashed without spinning out: five months and eighteen nights. Coincidentally, the same amount of time since he'd met Emilia.

And now, stretching and feeling muscles that, with time to rest, decided to remind him how overworked they were, he actually felt…good. Not as tired. Maybe a little energetic.

Well, at least energetic enough to cuddle with his fiancée. He slid against her compact frame, her naked back pressed against his bare chest. The warmth emanating from her stoked a flame that was pretty much always lit around her. Blood and lust pooled south of his waist, and he rocked into her, eliciting a moan from Emilia.

God, how he wanted this woman. Every hour of every day, his need for her grew. It didn't hurt that she was carrying a life inside her made from their shared desire.

Wrapping a hand around her waist and clasping her hips, he drew her tight against him so his erection slipped between her legs. He traced the soft swell of her belly up to full, swollen breasts. He cupped them, gently massaging the firm, suppleness in the hopes it would wake his sleeping bride-to-be so they could start their day off with what he'd been dreaming about all night.

It was nice to see Emilia relaxed all evening, even if she'd seemed a little preoccupied. But when she'd sighed, slipping out of the new cerulean robe he'd given her at the end of the night... All he'd wanted was to kiss every inch of her gorgeous, curvy frame. But he'd promised her sleep, and hell, he'd needed to catch up on the elusive stuff, too. Now, though, the hunger for her roared in his chest, waking him up better than any espresso could.

Emilia didn't stir, and as his hand settled on her chest, it felt more than warm. It was hot. He placed the inside of his wrist along her forehead, and it burned. She had a fever.

Dammit. How had he missed that? He jumped out of bed and raced to find a thermometer, throwing on his sweats from the night before on the way to the bathroom. It didn't take him long to find the medical supplies under the bathroom sink. When he got back to her bedside, Emilia's skin was damp and clammy. He pulled back the sheet, and she shivered, but her eyes didn't open. She was burning up, though. As he tried to roll the thermometer across her forehead, she groaned and shifted.

And Aiodhán froze, fear seizing his chest and each cell in his limbs. Blood. Not a lot, but enough that it meant something was wrong. It had stained a small circle of the sheets and her skin on her thighs, but it might as well have been a bucket of the stuff the way it filled Aiodhán with dread.

"Chance!" Aiodhán shouted. The man stormed in like he'd been waiting just outside the door.

"What is it?" One glance at Emilia and his face lost its color. "What happened?"

"She's bleeding, and her pulse is erratic. I need you to call her parents. Have them meet us at Minnie Gen."

"Shouldn't I call for an ambulance?"

"No time." Aiodhán already had Emilia in his arms, a nightgown covering her slight frame. "I can get her there quicker."

Chance blanched when he saw the spot on the bed where Emilia was. Aiodhán swallowed hard and grabbed his keys.

"Is she—" Chance asked.

"I don't know. It's not enough yet, but if we don't figure out what's going on, it'll be bad."

What if...?

No. He couldn't think that way. His only focus was Emilia's health. And the baby's, hopefully.

"I'll drive. You make sure she lives," Chance said. Aiodhán nodded, tossing him the keys as they all but ran out of the apartment.

The drive to the hospital was short—made quicker by Chance's expert maneuvering of the city streets—but it still felt interminable. Emilia was in and out of awareness, and her skin was hot, pale, and damp. Not good signs.

As Chance tore into the ER entrance, Aiodhán

was out of the car with Emilia in his arms before the car could fully stop.

"Meet me inside," he yelled to Chance. He didn't turn around to make sure the man heard him, just raced inside the doors as fast as they'd open for him.

"We need help," he yelled. "Now!"

Nurses, residents on call, and Mallory came rushing to the entrance when they heard Aiodhán's booming voice.

"What happened?" Mallory asked, already putting a stethoscope on Emilia's chest as Aiodhán gingerly placed Emilia on a gurney. Memories of doing something similar just weeks ago sent a storm of grief crashing against Aiodhán's fortitude.

This. This was his greatest fear realized. Had he made it happen by being too greedy, too happy?

"She was unresponsive this morning. Running a hundred-and-two fever, thready pulse."

"Okay. Anything else I need to know before I do a workup?"

"I'll come with you and assist."

"You're too close, Aiodhán. You're her fiancé." His chin hit his chest with blunt force. He nodded his agreement. "How far along?"

"Twenty-three weeks." Far enough that he'd felt safe. She'd been doing so well.

She offered him a gentle pat on the shoulder, a paltry consolation to the fear mounting in his mind.

"How bad is the bleeding?"

"Light, but enough to bleed through her undergarments." Aiodhán's voice cracked, along with his composure.

"I need to take her now, but I'll take good care of your family."

Emilia just looked so…small. The woman herself was a beacon of strength in every way—taking care of patients, of him—all with a smile on her face despite her own exhaustion. Yet, as the shell of her human form lay there, lifelessly being rolled toward a trauma room, she appeared fragile for the first time.

"Please. She's…she's everything to me."

Mallory nodded and jogged after the gurney carrying the only things Aiodhán cared about. He looked around the waiting room, and his chest ached. What he should do is get to work so he could distract himself from the crippling dread. But how the actual hell was he supposed to give a patient his best self when the best of him was in a trauma ward being poked and prodded while she tried to live and keep their child alive at the same time?

No, work was off the table, but just as terrifying was waiting. Because it allowed the doubt to creep in and take root in his chest, making it hard to breathe. Faced with losing Emilia, their baby or, God forbid, both, he couldn't believe he ever cared about work or anything as menial. Because he'd give it all up if doing so would ensure her safety and health.

But that's not how it worked, so all he could do now was wait. Wait and hope that everything he loved wasn't ripped from him again. Because no amount of surgeries or saves would make up for what losing Emilia would cost him.

Aiodhán tapped his feet on the tile floor with impatience. He'd paced the entire lobby and every place the staff allowed him to be. He'd checked in with Mallory who told him Emilia was taken into surgery—all she was able to tell him because, injustice of all injustices, she still wasn't his wife.

It wasn't for a lack of trying. But now, twelve hours before their wedding, he was in a standstill hoping she *lived*, let alone could become his wife.

So he waited for news, or her parents to arrive, or the chance to see her. Chance had some issues contacting the king and queen since they were at the governor's mansion and all phones had been relinquished.

"This is asinine," he muttered.

"There are so many ways your language fails you, Dr. Adler, but in this case, I'm inclined to agree. Might there be a way we can find what we're looking for without the traditional means?"

"You mean sneak up to her room?"

"I wouldn't dream of suggesting such a thing. However, you should do what you think best, and I would happily support the future prince consort's efforts from here."

Aiodhán chuckled, the levity a welcome respite. The man had bugged him at first, but now it was nice having a sidekick in his efforts to keep the princess safe.

Fat lot of good it'd done any of them. Emilia was right, per usual. There wasn't much anyone could control when it came to keeping loved ones safe in a fast-paced world like they lived in.

But where he'd really been wrong? Believing that keeping himself separated from anything resembling love would prevent him from being hurt. Sure, he'd been unattached and content, but he hadn't been *happy* before Emilia. And he wouldn't trade knowing her, no matter the outcome.

"Okay. I'm gonna…go check on a surgical patient upstairs. If her parents get here, you'll call me?"

"Of course," Chance replied. He looked as stoic as ever, but Aiodhán knew the man by now and caught the glint of mischief in his eyes.

Aiodhán didn't waste a minute. He took the back stairs by the employee entrance to the fourth floor, the OB surgical suites. Ducking his head, he circumvented the staff until he found the surgery board behind the nurses' station.

His pulse raced as he found what he was looking for.

E. de Reyes. Premature labor. Room three.

Oh, God. Premature labor. A miscarriage most likely. He inhaled deeply, the cool air doing not a damn thing to keep the tears—hot and heavy—from burning the backs of his eyes. A few fell, but he couldn't let the pain itching beneath his skin out. His job was to be there for Emilia.

Closing his hands into tight fists, Aiodhán made his way to Emilia's recovery room. Mallory's voice drifted into the hallway, calm but hushed.

Aiodhán ducked behind the wall. She wouldn't appreciate his subterfuge to come up against her advice. But she didn't get it. Emilia was his world. Supporting her through this was too damn important to bring nuance into it. He might not be her husband—yet—but that didn't mean she wasn't his world.

"You're still on bed rest. Premature labor puts the mother through hell, Emilia. You need to heal."

Aiodhán clamped his eyes shut. Nothing about the baby.

"What about…what about having children later?"

"Let's not worry about that right now. Our focus is on your health and getting you through this. Okay? I'm going to get a couple labs ordered, but I'll be back soon."

"Thank you, Mallory. Um, can I ask you something?"

"Sure." Aiodhán leaned in to hear what Emilia asked.

"Can you not tell my parents or Aiodhán what's going on? I'd like to talk to them myself."

"Of course."

Aiodhán turned his head as Mallory passed by, issuing orders to one of her interns. She didn't see him as he slipped around the corner and into the room where Emilia lay, facing the window. Her face was turned from him, but he could see the shine of tears on her cheeks. All he wanted to do was run to her, to take her home and hold her while she healed on his watch.

That feeling was amplified when she turned to look at him.

"Aiodhán," she whispered. He moved to the edge of the bed, which was topped with at least a dozen blankets and pillows. It only served to make Emilia look smaller, more tender and breakable. But she was still there, and he sent up a silent prayer to whomever was in charge of such things in the universe that she was safe.

He couldn't process the potential loss of their child, wouldn't go there yet, not if he needed to be there for Emilia. They could cross that bridge later, when they'd both grieved and settled back into their jobs and new marriage.

"What are you doing here?" she asked him. He wiped a tear with the pad of his thumb.

"I couldn't wait to see you. No one was telling me anything, and I was so scared."

"I'm fine, Aiodhán."

"I'm so damn glad you're okay. I was so scared." He kissed her. "And the baby—"

Her hand fluttered to her abdomen.

"It's okay. We don't need to talk about the baby now. Or the wedding, or the move. We can just let you heal." He didn't care how hurt he was: he'd be strong for her if it was the last thing he did. "I'll make sure you get to stay here and practice medicine, and you don't have to go back if you don't want to. Hell, you don't have to get married if it'll keep you here. Just tell me what you want."

Tell me what will take the pain of losing our daughter and smooth it into something we can live with.

The look on her face—vacant with a faraway stare—combined with the sweet, simple gesture of reaching for the swell in her stomach cracked his chest open for her. She'd lost so much.

"Aiodhán," she said, looking at him again.

"Yeah, Em?"

"The baby is okay. For now. I got a cervical cerclage that should help."

He felt the relief as it spread to his limbs. A sob escaped his chest. He squeezed her hand, but she pulled back.

"Oh, thank God. I was so petrified—"

"You weren't ever going to get married, were you?"

Shock twisted his lips in confusion. "What do you mean?"

"Before you met me. You were happy at work, with your career and not dating or getting involved with anyone."

"That's true, sort of, but—"

"And the baby shifted everything. It shifted things that shouldn't be moved. You are who you are, and this baby didn't change that." That wasn't true. He *had* changed. And it wasn't the baby, it was Emilia. Sure, the baby had woken him up to just how much

Emilia meant to him, but he loved her for who she was to him.

"Maybe at first, but…" He drew a breath he hoped would fortify him. "I love you. It showed me that."

"Enough to move to Zephyranthes and lead a life tied to the monarchy? Because that's still the plan, you know. For me to go back. I *want* to go back. It's my duty, but it's a part of who I am. I'm raising our daughter in Zephyranthes."

"Okay, then we'll talk about it sooner. I'll take the advisory position until we can work out the challenges with my medical practice. Whatever it takes."

Emilia shut her eyes, and the overpowering desire to kiss her pressed against his heart. But it wasn't the right time. Not when she was struggling with almost losing a pregnancy and what it all would mean.

"Aiodhán, you say you love me, but the woman you see here isn't the same woman who is duty bound to Zephyranthes. Here, I can laugh and be free and eat takeout with you. But there? I'm a princess, Aiodhán, and if you don't like the king and queen, you won't much like your wife."

"You don't know that." His hands shook now.

"I do. It's why Luis sold my secrets. It was easier to betray the crown than marry into it. So I'm letting you off the hook. I don't need you to go through with this wedding for me or the baby. I'll take care of my parents and the press. You go back to being the man I fell in love with, the man who is going to save so many people's lives."

Aiodhán stood up, his mouth open in protest.

Mallory came into the room, stopping the words that sat thick on his tongue, waiting for a way out.

"Okay, Emilia—" She took one look at Aiodhán and frowned. "What are you doing here?"

"Mallory, you know damn well that rule isn't for people like us. I need to talk to my fiancée." They needed a few more minutes, a respite where he could gain his bearings and they could talk this out. There had to be some middle ground he was missing.

"Fine. You can stay if the patient agrees."

"Are my parents here?" Emilia asked, ignoring Aiodhán's desperate, wordless plea. Mallory nodded. "Can you send them up? I'd like to tell them what's happening."

"You bet. I'll ring downstairs and have them sent up."

Emilia turned to Aiodhán, the tears falling freely on her cheeks now.

"That's it, Aiodhán. We tried, and you were wonderful. But I don't need you to cover for me anymore. The rest I have to do on my own."

Breathing was all of a sudden difficult. Letting go of her hand impossible.

"You can't think that just because we lived different lives before we met—"

"That's exactly what I think. And it doesn't mean I don't love you. Because I do and probably always will, Aiodhán." Her voice broke, spilling emotion into the sterile room.

"Just not enough to do this with me."

"So much I'd never drag you through this with

me if there was a way to let you live the life you'd planned for yourself. This is it. You're free."

"And if I don't want to be free? If I want you?"

She settled her gaze on the window again. "You don't want to be the prince consort of Zephyranthes, and in marrying me, that would be your fate. Do you want that?"

He squeezed her hand. "There has to be another way. When we found out we were pregnant—"

"The baby was a delay. This was always going to be the outcome. I go home and rule my country with my parents by my side. Our baby is royalty, whether we like it or not. She can come stay with you from time to time, but her place is in Zephyranthes, too. You stay here and save lives."

"You can't say goodbye just because we've had a hard time—"

"Please don't make this harder than it already is for me, Aiodhán," she said. "We don't work outside of the one thing that flung us together in the first place. Even then, we were struggling to blend our lives so much that it was killing both of us. It almost killed our child."

"So, what do you want from me?"

She glanced back at him, her tear-stained cheeks an ache that wouldn't abate.

"I want you to go, to make yourself happy and fulfilled again, and to let me do the same from home."

"Home? You mean Zephyranthes? You won't even stay so I can meet our child?"

"I can't stay in this place and be reminded of everything I want that keeps being pulled just out of reach. The universe is telling me to let you go, and everything that comes with that. Besides, I can't practice surgery like this. I'm on partial bed rest. What use would I be?"

Aiodhán opened his mouth to argue, when Emilia's parents ran in. Rebecca looked scared, and Emilia's father as if he might cry. Aiodhán understood.

"Good-bye, Aiodhán," she said, turning her focus to her parents.

He walked out of the room, but there wasn't a cell in his body that could tell Emilia goodbye. Not if he expected to walk out of this place in one piece. She'd said she was giving him back the life he'd planned, but he didn't want it. Maybe he never had: it'd been a coward's way out, and Emilia had showed him how to be brave and long for more.

It was then he realized the hardest part of loving someone. It was hard to cope with the loss of them unexpectedly, and she'd been right that he couldn't control that, nor should he try.

But harder still—impossible, even—was the idea that he could lose the two things he loved most, and both of them would still be out in the world, living without him.

She might have to let him go, but he'd never be able to release Emilia de Reyes from the hold she had on his heart.

Never.

CHAPTER NINETEEN

EMILIA DE REYES might be gone, but damn if Aiodhán didn't see her ghost everywhere. The alluring combination of vanilla and coffee seemed ingrained in his clothes, even though her side of the closet comprised just a few empty hangers.

Call him crazy, but he swore he heard her laughter ringing down the halls when he was in the main campus of the hospital. And then there was the way everyone looked at him like *he* was the ghost. Like he was fragile and might disappear at any moment. That was, when they didn't actively avoid him.

The only people in his corner were Mallory and Brian.

"Have you heard from her?" Brian asked over a beer the second week after Emilia had packed up and went back to Zephyranthes.

Aiodhán took a long pull from the bottle of amber. It tasted sour, but then, so did everything these days.

"Not a thing. And I won't. She said goodbye, man, and for the life of me, I'm not sure what I should do with that."

Brian gave him a sideways glance. "What's there to do but the usual? Throw yourself into the clinic, into your patients, and wait for the sting to wear off. I'm happy to tell dad jokes if you're up to hearing them."

Aiodhán chuckled, shaking his head. "Nah, but

thanks. And don't think I haven't tried the usual. But can I tell you something? Something you have to keep to yourself?"

"Of course. But in the spirit of full disclosure, I can't keep anything from Mal. Believe me, I've tried, but it's like the minute we got married, I couldn't wait to tell her everything and anything."

A small twinge of jealousy tweaked Aiodhán's heart, leaving behind a dull ache. He understood completely. Because he felt the same way about Emilia. She'd been his person, the one he wanted to share every mundane case from work or silly idea for decorating the trauma waiting room with, and everything in between.

"I figured. That's fine."

"So…spill."

Aiodhán glanced across the spacious living room of Emilia's penthouse. She'd left with almost ten months remaining on the lease and invited Aiodhán to stay and use the space since his closet-sized apartment in the lower downtown wasn't exactly comfortable. He hadn't planned on taking her up on it, but how could he leave? Especially when an overwhelming part of him hoped he'd come home from work one day and find her there in the living room, her growing belly propping up a book while she sipped the decaf coffee she was never without.

"I don't want to work."

Brian's mouth dropped open. Aiodhán didn't blame the guy for his surprise. The realization had hit *him* like a ton of bricks falling from a ten-story building.

"I'm sorry, who are you, and what have you done with my best friend? You don't want to work? The one thing that's driven you since we met in med school?"

"I know. It's not like I don't love medicine and helping patients anymore. But the clinic and the extra hours and the chasing down some magical elixir that'll erase decades of guilt... None of it worked. The only thing that's actually made me happy was Emilia."

"Even knowing you'd be marrying into some crazy royal drama?"

"Even then. Especially then. Watching her navigate that and still pursue her dreams was inspiring as hell. It made me think..."

He shook his head, drank down a third of his beer.

"What?"

"It made me think I've been prioritizing all the wrong things my whole life. And I want a do-over."

Mallory sipped her drink, a pink cocktail in a rocks glass, a half smile tugging at the corner of her mouth.

"I know. I'm just glad you finally figured it out."

"What?" Brian asked. His eyes were as wide as his open mouth. "Am I the only one here surprised by this turn of events?"

"Yes," Mallory and Aiodhán replied in unison.

"You love her, and love changes your mind and heart when it comes to deciding what's important."

"Yeah, but what good does all that do?" Aiodhán asked. He got up and went to the window overlooking his city. It didn't feel like home anymore, not since the best part about it skipped town and crossed the Atlantic. "She's gone and told me to shove off. The thing is, I get it now. How hard I tried to keep it all together when all I really wanted was to be with her. How it looked when I only let her know how much she meant to me when I found out about the pregnancy. The medicine would always come back around when I needed it, but her? I lost that chance."

He couldn't talk about their daughter: it was too damned hard to think about. Being a father was never on the table until it was dropped there in front of him, and now he couldn't imagine his child growing up without getting to be a part of every single moment. But losing the love of his life to his own stupidity took that chance with it as well.

"Would you give it up to be with her?"

Aiodhán barked out a humorless laugh. "I already have, even if it doesn't do any good."

"What do you mean?" Mallory asked.

"I handed over the clinic to Bob Thomas. He's been vying to be involved since it's been up and running, and to be honest he's a better fit over there where he won't have any interns to pretend to teach. I just want a life of helping people for the sake of helping people, and to hell with the tally. Emilia was right—that was never within my control. My parents lost their lives, but I'm not giving mine up out of guilt or some misplaced sense of playing God."

The silence behind him wasn't as disconcerting as the whispers that followed. He spun around, and the couple broke apart like they'd been caught at something nefarious. All Aiodhán caught was a hissed "No. It's patient confidentiality" from Brian.

"What's supposed to be kept confidential?" Aiodhán asked. Brian stared at Mallory, whose gaze was pinned to Aiodhán's. Brian shook his head, finally relenting and falling back against the couch. "If you two know something and you aren't telling me...so help me I'll never forgive either of you."

"You want this to work, right?" Mallory asked.

"I do. More than anything else. I mean, I gave up the one thing I've been working on my whole career, if that's any indication."

"Okay, then you need to call her parents. Talk to them and see how you can make it work. Because I know you, Aiodhán, and you can love Emilia all day long, but if you don't have something that's yours, you'll go crazy. They can help with that."

"How are you so sure they'll want to help me with anything? I mean, I let their pregnant daughter leave here without a fight."

She shrugged, sipping her pink drink like she was the royal. "I got to know them pretty well while they were here taking care of Emilia. They only want her to be happy, Ad. And you made her happy."

"Would..." He struggled to find a way to articulate the swirl of thoughts buzzing in his head. "Would Emilia hate me for that?"

"My guess is no," Mallory said, her smile as wide as it had been on her wedding day. It was a flotation device while he was drowning. "She misses you."

"Mallory," Brian exhaled at the same time Aiodhán said, *"What?"*

"It's not patient confidentiality when this had nothing to do with her surgery," Mallory said, kissing her husband until the shock made way for a contented smile.

"How the hell do you know how she feels? Are you still talking to her?"

"Okay, since my lovely better half can't keep anything to herself, she's right. Emilia's been checking in on you, wants to know how you're doing and all that."

Aiodhán got up and paced in front of the couch. "But she left me."

"No. She thought you were only marrying her because of the baby, and she gave you an out. You're the one who took it."

"Dammit. Well, I'm untaking it."

"I mean what I said, Ad. You need to make sure you have a plan before you jet across the ocean with nothing but love in your suitcase. Upending both your lives will take more than that."

"Oh, I know. And for the first time in my life, I'm more than a little sure what *I* want and that the work will be worth it."

Mallory's smile turned soft like it did when she looked at Brian.

"Then, go get her," she said. Brian's arm wrapped

around his wife's waist, and he pulled her into a deep kiss as Aiodhán strode to the closet, whipped out a suitcase, and started throwing stuff in it. For the first time, he didn't resent the extra minutes in the elevator or waiting on labs that he had spent practicing his Zephyr. He'd need it, now.

"If you two lovebirds are done making out, I could use your help getting a ride to the airport so I can make a call that's long overdue."

CHAPTER TWENTY

EMILIA PACED THE marble floor of her suite, unable to concentrate on the beauty of the cerulean sea beneath her. It met the pale yellow sand of the shoreline with gentle caresses, the sound of the water's crashing and receding dance usually calming. But not today.

No, today, her focus was pulled to the meeting her parents had set up for her. She'd been expecting it since she'd arrived back in Zephyranthes, the thick, salty sea air greeting her like an old friend. Part of her was delighted to be back in her home country—especially since she'd be keeping up with her medical studies in the Hospitál Real de Cyana—the Royal Cyana Hospital.

She'd been surprised when her stepmother suggested it and even more shocked when Rebecca made the king see how necessary it was for Emilia to continue her studies—both for her country and her well-being.

It'd brought her a measure of pride to know her father was still growing as a leader and a man she could look up to.

But she'd left behind her heart in Aiodhán, which she wouldn't need here, anyway, it seemed. It was time to take a suitor and fill the role she'd been born into. At least that's why she assumed she was being called to the Great Hall by her parents. Why else would they ask her to dress befitting her role and, Rebecca had added, wear those earrings she'd received from her stepmother as an engagement present in Minneapolis?

Her stomach rolled with disgust as she got ready. It didn't matter who they'd picked because it wasn't Aiodhán Adler, the love of her life and father of the precious child she carried. But if she made waves about this, would they strip her of her internship?

Did it matter? Yes. To the people—the women and children—she'd save, yes, it mattered.

Even if…

The throbbing ache in her chest hadn't abated since her plane had landed in Zephyranthes. If anything, it grew each day, each moment she went without Aiodhán's crooked smile shining down on her, without his arms pulling her close, without his lips grazing hers and making her feel like it would all be okay.

She'd marry, she'd practice medicine and rule her country when it was time for her to take over, but there wouldn't be a breath she took that wasn't laced with regret and grief at what that life would cost her and her daughter.

A knock on the heavy oak door of her suite roused her from her bout of self-pity.

"Come in," she commanded. The door opened to her father and stepmother, her father dressed in military blues and Rebecca a cream gown that showed off her grace, elegance, and beauty. Would Emilia, clad in a jade gown Rebecca chose for her, ever feel that natural in this space?

Maybe she would have with Aiodhán by her side, but alone she felt adrift and every bit a royal impostor. Being a doctor and Aiodhán's fiancée were the only times she'd truly felt at home in her own skin. She could have ruled the world with him by her side.

"Are you ready?" they asked. She nodded, even though it took every ounce of her strength to perform that simple gesture. Her footsteps grew heavier with each one she took.

They led the way out of the living chambers and to the Great Hall. She'd always loved the regal space as a child, with its grand painted ceilings and the molding from centuries before her time. But now it felt like a well-adorned prison cell, a frozen space where her life would cease to carry meaning.

Throwing her shoulders back and her chin up, she strode into the room as if this wasn't the last day of the rest of her life she'd be free to love another man, even from afar.

She could see the tuft of brown hair in the chair reserved for guests at the formal table in the center of the hall, and her chest cracked open, spilling out thoughts of the man she loved, a man a million miles from where she was. The espresso-colored waves only reminded her of Aiodhán.

"Your Royal Highness, Princess Emilia de Reyes of Zephyranthes, may we present to you your betrothed."

So it was true. She was to marry. Even suspecting it didn't cushion the blow. She would never love him like she loved Aiodhán...

The man stood up and turned to face her.

The eyes gazing back at her were the same eyes that had captured her interest seven months ago and her heart not long after that. They broke through whatever fears she'd built into a fortifying wall, and they came crashing down around her.

"Aiodhán," she whispered, "you're here."

"There weren't many paparazzi to greet me, either," he said jokingly. "I could get used to that."

His gaze fell to her abdomen, which had grown considerably now that she was in her third trimester. He took a tentative step toward her, and her hands trembled with anticipation.

"I could get used to this, too. She's grown."

She nodded her head, which was still fuzzy with disbelief. Aiodhán was in her home, sitting at her dining table, looking every bit like he belonged there. Her heart almost couldn't handle the stress of her dreams coming true. She could show him her birthplace, her birthright... She could kiss him in plain daylight for the world to see. He could hold their daughter when she was born and every day after.

She hoped.

Wait—her parents had said *betrothed*, hadn't they?

Tears pricked the back of her eyes that she wouldn't dare blame on the mess of hormones coursing through her veins. They were tears of happiness, nothing more.

"Well, my dear, we'll leave you two to discuss your future and how you'd like to proceed. But Emilia?"

"Yes, Father?" Her voice sounded far away, muffled under a million questions.

"We've given Dr. Adler our blessing and want you to have the same."

She nodded, her gaze still on Aiodhán—*there! In her home!*—until Rebecca's hand fell on her shoulder.

"You should know I'll be opening an art gallery as well. It will have a space dedicated to teach art classes to children whose circumstances wouldn't allow it before. I wanted you to know you're the reason I'll finally chase my own dreams. Thank you, Emilia."

Emilia could only smile and hug her stepmother before her parents left, leaving her alone with Aiodhán. So much information was shared with her in the past few moments she wasn't sure where to start.

"Aiodhán," she said, walking toward him. He'd crossed the Atlantic for her; it was the least she could do to meet him where he stood. "You're here."

"You said that already."

They shared a laugh before he grew serious.

"I am. And as long as you'll have me, I'm here to stay."

Her smile twisted with concern.

"But your job—"

"I talked the board into giving control of the clinic to Dr. Thomas before I talked to Mal and Brian." He took her hands in his and brought them to his lips. Her heart fluttered like a thousand butterflies were trapped inside it. "I gave over my service to Mal, and she'll take on the role of chief now that I'm gone." He kissed her knuckles, sending a flash of heat straight to Emilia's stomach.

"Oh," was all Emilia was capable of saying. She swallowed. "Why did you do that? Your life and practice are in Minneapolis. I know meeting me steered you off course."

The subtle shake of his head made Emilia's mouth go dry.

"Meeting you didn't steer me off course, Emilia. It changed my course. *You're* my life—everything that matters in it, anyway. And my practice is now as a general surgeon in the... Real Hospital in Cyana?"

She laughed. "Hospitál Real de Cyana?" she asked.

"Yeah. That."

"But...why?"

Aiodhán released her hands only to draw her into an embrace that gave her strength. *Dío*, how she'd missed that. Missed this man who, she had to admit, pulled off his gray seersucker suit very nicely.

"Because no number of people I save will matter if I don't save myself. When I took a look—a real, honest, hard look—at myself, I realized only one thing mattered. Well, two actually."

"What were they?" she asked. Aiodhán dipped down, his lips brushing hers.

"You. And this little bean." He laid his hand on her belly, and as if on cue, the baby kicked. "Was that her?"

"It was. It seems she likes hearing such sweet words from her father."

"I like hearing you call me that. But she's not the reason I proposed to you. When you woke up on the table after hitting your head that day in the hospital, I knew I wanted to be with you and keep you safe—" She opened her mouth to protest, but he kissed her silent. "Just a sec. I have to get this out. I know now I can't control that, so I want to make you a new proposal."

"First, how did you get the job at *el hospital*? Not the adviser?"

He laughed. "My headstrong princess. Your parents offered it to me. Apparently, when your girlfriend is the princess, the king pulls special favors. They were looking for a trauma surgeon, and he said he knew a guy. They rushed the reciprocity of my medical license."

Emilia was mildly annoyed they hadn't done that earlier but understood their reticence. Her parents had stuck their necks out to support Emilia and Aiodhán and had wanted to know they were committed to one another.

"So you're really here? And you're okay with…" she spread her arms to indicate the castle they stood at the center of "…all this?"

"If it comes with you at the end of the day, I'm excited to take it on. Plus, it seems like the trauma center idea sounded good to the hospital board, so I'll be building one up here. Would you do me the honor of creating it with me?"

"I would love that, Aiodhán."

He released her, though, and the inches separating them brought a layer of cold that hadn't been in the room before. Until he dipped to one knee, and her skin flushed again.

"Now for the proposal. I want to grow old as long as we have together. I want to love you every day like I'll lose you tomorrow and celebrate every day we're given. The pregnancy might have brought you to me, but we're choosing this life together from here forward. Or at least, I am."

She'd thought the same thing when she'd been on her way to her bachelorette party with Bridget. That seemed like a thousand years ago. She nodded, unable to speak.

"Okay, then, now on to the important question." Aiodhán drew a small oak box from his pocket, and when he opened it to reveal a princess-cut diamond the size of her knuckle, she gasped. Not at the ring, which was stunning, yes, but at the love pooling along the edges of the eyes of the man offering it to her.

"Yes!" she said.

"Well, that's the answer I was hoping for. But I haven't even asked the question yet."

They both laughed, and she wiped a stray tear from her cheek.

"Emilia de Reyes, Dr. de Reyes… Will you do me the honor of being my partner in medicine and in life? I want to raise kids and travel and practice medicine and even drink that stuff you call coffee every day with you, for the rest of our lives. So, what do you say? You in?"

She smiled, and the kick from their daughter giving her own version of an answer filled Emilia's heart more than it was already.

"Yes, I am. Every day for the rest of time."

Aiodhán swooped her up in an embrace and kissed her thoroughly, the taste of vanilla and promise on his lips. Her parents strode in, shouting congratulations as Emilia let the truth of it all settle on her heart.

She wasn't going to get everything she'd ever wanted—she already had it all.

EPILOGUE

A year later

EMILIA ROCKED NORA, named after her mother, humming a Zephyr lullaby.

"There's the two most beautiful women on earth. I've been looking all over the castle for you."

Emilia smiled and leaned in for a kiss. The passion that blazed when her lips met Aiodhán's still surprised her. She didn't see a day that she'd ever tire of wanting the man.

"I wanted to show her the sunset over her country now that she's finally old enough to be awake for it."

"You mean you walked her all over the castle and she still didn't fall asleep?"

Emilia laughed. Aiodhán held out his arms to take their daughter, and she begrudgingly handed sweet Nora over.

"It took four hours of walking and singing. I've run out of melodies to hum. I daresay I'm excited to take my exams tomorrow, so I'll give my voice a break." Emilia was getting certified as a neonatal surgeon tomorrow, if everything went well. Then, she'd be a colleague to the hottest doctor she'd ever met.

"I think our little princess must be as lively as her mother."

"*Sí,*" Emilia agreed, starting the long walk back from the grotto overlooking the Mediterranean. "I do love this view, though," she said, gazing out over her country. Aiodhán smiled.

His gaze was fixed on her. "So do I."

The fire in her stomach rolled and burned, flooding her with need.

"Let's drop her off with Sofie," Emilia told him. "I'd like some time alone with you."

His brow raised, letting her know he appreciated the thought.

"I promise I won't fall asleep, no matter how many melodies you hum me, my love. As long as you keep those lips on mine."

She winked at him, marveling at how in love with her life she was. She'd enjoy all of it as it came to her. Right now, that meant giving her attention to her husband, the love of her life and chief of surgery at their hospital.

She had plans for him that didn't involve sleep.

Tomorrow she'd delight in making the rest of her dreams come true. As fairy tales went, hers really was the sweetest.

* * * * *

*If you enjoyed this story,
check out these other great reads
from Kristine Lynn*

A Kiss with the Irish Surgeon
Their Six-Month Marriage Ruse
Accidentally Dating His Boss
Brought Together by His Baby

All available now!